If you want to find out . . .

How Hedley Hopkins Did a Dare,

robbed a grave,

made a new friend who might not really have been there at all,

and while he was at it

committed a

terrible sin

which everyone was doing

even though he

didn't know it

. . . read this book!

How Hedley Hopkins Did a Dare,

robbed a grave,

made a new friend who might
not really have been there at all,

and while he was at it

committed a

terrible si

which everyone was doing
even though he
didn't know it

PUFFIN BOOKS

Published by the Penguin Group
Penguin Books Ltd, 80 Strand, London WC2R 0RL, England
Penguin Group (USA) Inc., 375 Hudson Street, New York, New York 10014, USA
Penguin Group (Canada), 90 Eglinton Avenue East, Suite 700, Toronto,
Ontario, Canada M4P 2Y3 (a division of Pearson Penguin Canada Inc.)
Penguin Ireland, 25 St Stephen's Green, Dublin 2, Ireland (a division of Penguin Books Ltd)
Penguin Group (Australia), 250 Camberwell Road, Camberwell, Victoria 3124, Australia
(a division of Pearson Australia Group Pty Ltd)
Penguin Books India Pvt Ltd, 11 Community Centre, Panchsheel Park,
New Delhi – 110 017, India
Penguin Group (NZ), cnr Airborne and Rosedale Roads, Albany, Auckland 1310,
New Zealand (a division of Pearson New Zealand Ltd)
Penguin Books (South Africa) (Pty) Ltd, 24 Sturdee Avenue, Rosebank,
Johannesburg 2196, South Africa

Penguin Books Ltd, Registered Offices: 80 Strand, London WC2R 0RL, England

www.penguin.com

First published in Australia by Penguin Group (Australia)
a division of Pearson Australia Group 2005
First published in Great Britain in Puffin Books 2005

1

Text copyright © Lockley Lodge Pty Ltd, 2005
All rights reserved

The moral right of the author has been asserted

Set in Sabon

British Library Cataloguing in Publication Data
A CIP catalogue record for this book is available from the British Library

ISBN 0–141–32043–5

contents

to
JULIE WATTS
CATHERINE McCREDIE
KATIE EVANS

My wonderful publisher and editors.
Thank you so much for the ideas,
the encouragement, the research and the
many, many careful and loving edits.
I can never thank you enough for
helping me tell this story.

1

half-moon murderers

THEY SAY THERE is something awful in the sand dunes.

Kate and I walk along the beach kicking seaweed and looking at stuff that has been washed up. There is not a single footprint in the sand, which means that no one has been along this way since high tide. There might be something good amongst the seaweed. So far we have only found a broken lobster pot and a dead penguin with no eyes.

It is a lonely beach with a lonely sky.

The sand dunes are covered in marram grass. Huge waves thunder up the beach and then run out of puff.

The waves are powerful but they can't hurt you unless you get too close. Of course you never know when an extra big one is going to rush up and grab you. Life is like that. Just when you feel safe – *bang* – something awful happens. A wave of fate knocks you over.

'The grave's behind the Loony Bin,' says Kate.

The Loony Bin is where the mad people live. I have never seen them because there is a big wire fence around the whole place and thick bushes grow on the other side. But there are stories.

One night Ian Douglas told me about the loonies when I was walking home from Cubs. He kept walking behind me and I couldn't get rid of him.

'One of the loonies is a full-moon murderer,' he said in a fake scary voice. 'And he often gets out at night.'

'I'm not frightened of lunatics,' I said.

But that was a lie. As I walked along trying not to listen I looked up into the cold sky where the full moon was so bright that any murderer could see us just as if it was midday. Ian Douglas is a big tough kid and his house is close to the Church Hall where the Cubs meet. He turned into his front garden and laughed at something that I didn't know about. *He* didn't have to walk on his own after Cubs. But I did.

I was alone in the glare of the moon and it was a long way back to my house. Each driveway could have hidden a full-moon murderer. I walked down the centre of the road to give myself a chance if one jumped out. A few weeks later Ian Douglas told me that there are also *half*-moon murderers in the Loony Bin. The night he told me that, there just happened to be a half-moon and I was so scared I thought I was going to faint. When I finally got home, Mum and Dad and Kate were out. Probably gone for a walk around the block with Kate tagging along behind.

I wanted to jump into bed but a thought kept coming into my mind that a half-moon murderer might be hiding underneath. Once this thought comes into your mind you have to take a look. Otherwise you will lie there all night imagining a hand coming out and grabbing you. But if you look under the bed and see a face staring back, you will die of fright just from the terror of the experience. So I do my usual trick and roll a ball underneath. If it comes out the other side of the bed I am safe.

The ball did not come out the other side. It took me ages and ages to get up the courage to take a peek. There was no one under the bed. The ball had been stopped by a pair of underpants that I had kicked under there the week before. That's what I mean – *bang* – you are never safe from an unexpected wave of fate.

My parents make me sleep with the light out. I'm scared of the dark and I don't want it to be turned off.

'We're not wasting electricity when you're asleep,' says Mum.

Mum and Dad don't give a tinker's cuss about dark streets or shadows in your bedroom.

'In the Blitz we had total blackout,' said Dad. 'With Gerry bombers roaring over London.'

He is always talking about the War. He says that because food was short back in England when the War was on, they used to eat cats but I don't believe him.

'What did they taste like?' I asked him once.

'Rabbit,' he said. 'Couldn't tell the difference. Wasn't a cat to be seen in our neighbourhood, I can tell you that.' He gave a short laugh at this.

Parents don't seem to know what it is like to be a kid. They live in a different world. They are not scared of the dark and they laugh at strange things. Eating cats is not funny. Nor are half-moon murderers who might escape from the Loony Bin.

Kate and I keep walking along the beach. The morning wind is cold and strong and our hair lashes our eyes and cheeks. Our feet sink into the wet sand, which makes it hard going.

She is a good girl is our Kate but she is two years younger than me. I wish she was a boy and older but she isn't. If she was a boy I could play with her and no one would say anything. It is all right to play with a brother but not with a sister. At school you are a sissy if you play with your sister and it is not allowed by the other boys who will tease you if they see. But today it doesn't matter because we are alone on the beach as we walk towards the grave.

I have been going to school in Warrongbool for six months and still I do not have a bunch of kids to play with. It is hard to make friends. Everybody already has a friend. They are worried that their best friend will like you better than them and then they will be alone and not you. So I wander around at lunchtime with no one to talk to. I have to look as if I don't care. But I do.

Ian Douglas has a group of friends and they might let me join. You have to do a dare if you want to be in their group. If you don't do the dare then you are a chicken and there will be no hope for you ever. I'm worried about this. The dare could be something scary like doing a burglary or climbing inside the Loony Bin. I think I will have to do the dare, though. Then I'll have friends. Even if they are tough kids.

'It's up there,' says Kate pointing to a little track that winds up through the windswept grasses on the sand dunes.

'I know,' I say in an annoyed voice. Kate has to

realise that she is younger than me and I am the one who knows the way. But she doesn't seem to realise this. Kate is brave for her age.

The grave is not in a cemetery. It's all on its own in the sand dunes. No one seems to know who is buried there. It could have been someone who drowned when a convict ship sank off the reef many years ago. Probably a sailor. Maybe a soldier. Or the captain. It is a big grave with a concrete slab lying flat on top of it. All the letters have faded away except for part of a word – MANN.

We make our way to the top of the sand dune and look down on the grave. I gasp. So does Kate.

'It's true,' I say.

2

the coffin

THINGS HAVE CHANGED. The top of the grave is no longer covered. The slab of concrete has been moved to one side leaving a gaping black hole in the sand. For some reason it reminds me of the bloody space that is left after a tooth has been pulled out.

'Look at that,' whispers Kate.

I don't like this. Not one little bit. It's as if I have suddenly fallen into a dangerous world that I have only heard about on the wireless. In other countries there are wars and floods and gangsters and dead bodies. But in my world there are just school bullies and grazed knees and having your one-shilling pocket money stopped.

An open grave only happens in the pictures and I am shaking because this isn't the pictures. But I am Kate's big brother and I have to be tough.

'Come on,' I say as I roll up my sleeves. 'I'm going to have a look.'

My feet take me forward. I have had this feeling before. My brain doesn't want me to go. My heart is pounding with fear. But somehow my legs seem to have a life of their own. They just keep taking one step after another until I'm almost at the side of the grave.

It was the same the first time I jumped off the high diving board. I am scared of heights and I didn't want to do it. But all the kids who wanted to jump formed a line at the bottom of the ladder and I had to join them. Once I was in the line there was no way out. Up, up, up the ladder – one step after another to the platform. Then walking along the springboard to the edge. Oh, how I wanted to turn and go back. But I couldn't. Every boy in the school was watching. I closed my eyes and jumped. For a few long seconds I was in the air. Terror, nothing but terror. Then, *kersplash*. It was over.

Now I am at the edge of the grave. I can see the shape of the coffin at the bottom. It is not like the sort of coffins you see at funerals. This one is made of lead and has the body shape of the person who is inside.

Like an Egyptian mummy coffin but grey with no paintings or decoration.

Then I see something else.

A cold tingle of terror runs over my skin. What I see is not what I expect to see.

'What is it?' says Kate. She has crept up next to me but is staring up at the sky. She is sort of like the first person to reach a car crash. She wants to look but can't.

I just manage to scratch the words out with my dry tongue. 'A skull.'

Oh, horror. Oh, strike a light. Someone has been down into the grave and punched a hole through the lead coffin right above the place where the dead person's head would be. Next to the coffin, staring up at us with empty eyes, is a skull.

Kate half closes her eyes and finds the courage to peer over the edge. She screams in terror. I have never seen her scared like this before. Boy, does she run. She pelts over the dunes sending the sand shooting up from her heels like the spray from machine-gun bullets.

Suddenly I'm not the tough big brother. I give a scream of my own and scramble after Kate. We run like the Devil is on our tails. We belt along the wet sand close to the edge of the water where it's soggy but firmer than the dry sand further up. We send the seagulls screeching into the empty sky.

We don't notice the vast lonely sea. Or the lonely beach. The eye sockets of that terrible skull hold more loneliness than any heart can bear.

3

madness at midnight

KATE AND I thunder along the beach until we reach
the pier. There are people fishing and others just taking
a walk. Normal people. We are safe. But we still keep
running along the streets. We don't stop until we reach
our front garden.

We stagger inside and Kate and I fall into my bedroom and lie panting on the floor. Our chests hurt with
icy pains from all the running. At first we just gulp in
raw air and cannot talk from a shortage of breath.

Finally Kate manages to say, 'I'm telling Mum.'

'No,' I gasp. 'You mustn't. We're not allowed to
go near the Loony Bin. She'll go on and on about it

and we'll be in big trouble. And people might think *we* moved the slab from the grave.'

'No they wouldn't,' says Kate. 'It's too heavy. It would need men.'

'Or a gang of boys,' I say.

Somewhere at the back of my mind a black thought is gathering. This often happens to me. A thought is trying to escape. But something pushes it down and I become worried without knowing why. It's like putting the lid down on a . . . coffin.

'It was terrible,' gasps Kate. 'When I close my eyes I can still see it. It was real. A real, dead person's head.'

Most girls of Kate's age would start to cry. But she doesn't.

'Don't tell Mum,' I say.

'You're not the boss,' she says.

I have to be nice to her or she will tell everything. 'I know,' I say. 'But the skull can't hurt you. It can't move. It can't come here. Just forget about it. Someone will tell the Police and they'll put the slab back on top.'

'I don't like it,' says Kate.

'It's all right,' I say. 'We won't ever go there again.'

'Promise?' she says.

'Cross my heart and hope to die,' I say.

She needn't worry. There is nothing in the world that will make me go back to that grave.

Kate gets up and goes to her own room. I am alone with my thoughts. I start to talk to myself inside my head about what has happened.

The whole thing is hard to believe. It's the sort of story that you read about in comics like *Inner Sanctum* or *Tales of the Living Dead*. You don't find this sort of thing in *Blondie* and *Dagwood* comics which do not feature open graves.

Every boy at school collects comics to swap. You aren't allowed to take them to school so you have to smuggle them inside under your jumper. The most popular are *Superman*, *The Phantom* and *Donald Duck*. One coloured comic is worth three black-and-white ones. English comics like *Beano* and *Dandy*, which I like, are not worth much at all. American comics are the most popular. *Dagwood* and *Blondie* which are about the Bumstead family are funny. But I like them for another reason.

I take out a *Blondie* comic from where I have hidden it in the space under the bottom drawer of my desk. This will help me stop thinking about skulls. I start to trace over a picture of Blondie. I put my exercise book under the page and then I press hard over her outline in the comic with a roofing nail. I trace around her hair and face and her whole body including her breasts. But I don't trace around her blouse or slacks.

I go over the outline in my exercise book with a pencil and make a copy. Not an exact copy because my drawing of Blondie has no clothes on. She is stark naked. All I have to do is draw a little circle on each breast. These are the nipples which I colour in pink. I don't know what to draw where her legs join at the top so I just add a little bent line. If my mother ever found this exercise book the world would come to an end. My head would explode and blow all over the walls and there would be bits of brain and blood everywhere. And I would go to Hell and be tormented forever because I am drawing Blondie in the nude.

My mother does not like anything rude at all. I once got into terrible trouble at the table when we were eating cocktail sausages. 'Pass the frankfarts,' I said to Kate. Well, Mum went on and on and on about it. She kept looking at me as if I had stood up there and peed all over the table. Her looks can kill.

It's just as well that no one is listening to my thoughts. Staring at drawings of naked flesh is wicked. It makes me feel good in a bad way. Every time I do it, I say I will never do it again. But I always do. It is like being starving hungry and walking past a baker's shop. I can't think about anything else. I try and try and try but the thoughts about naked ladies just keep coming like the smell of fresh cakes.

Once when Mum and Dad and I were walking down the street at night I saw a book in the window of a shop. It was called *Madness at Midnight*. On the cover was a picture of a group of men in top hats standing around a dark and smoky stage. They were all staring up at a lady with no clothes on. I couldn't believe it. A real picture of a real lady with nothing on. Surely it was against the law. Even in 1956 you are not allowed to show such a thing in a shop. I couldn't stop looking at the picture. What was going on? What were those men doing there? They were in some dark and evil place like the inside of my mind. I longed to be there with them. I wanted to see what they could see. One of the top hats was in the way though, so I still couldn't see the bit at the top of the lady's legs. Mum and Dad didn't know what I was staring at. They were walking on ahead.

Every Friday night they go window shopping. Mum puts her arm through Dad's arm and they walk along looking at furniture and such like in the closed shops. They talk about what they would buy if they had the money. Chairs and curtains and things. They hardly know that I am there. Kate often stays at a friend's house so I follow like a forgotten dog that goes off and sniffs around on its own.

Kate has plenty of friends even though she is a Pommie like me. A Pommie is what Australian kids call someone from England. They say we talk funny. But for some reason it doesn't seem to matter to Kate's friends. They get together and play with their dolls and cane hoops. They put the hoops around their waists and wiggle so that the hoops spin around and don't fall to the ground. I sometimes try the hoop out in the back garden where no boys can see me.

I must be the only boy in the world who cannot stop thinking about naked ladies. All the others probably just dream about cricket and fishing and Biggles books. They are normal. I have been born very bad. I just can't help it. I have to get my mind on to something else.

Once again I see the grave and the skull in my mind. It seems to be calling me. I slap the side of my face to drive away the thought.

What I need is some friends to keep my mind off things. I am a dreamer and that is a problem – everyone says so. I will see if I can team up with Ian Douglas and his gang. Then I can muck around with normal boys and keep myself from thinking too much.

It will be worth it even if I have to do some terrible dare.

4

signing the pledge

IT IS SUNDAY and we all go to Church in the morning. I don't really like it much. The singing is all right but the sermons seem to go on and on forever. Also I don't really like wearing my best clothes. My shoes are shiny and my short pants have sharp creases in them. I have to wear a tie and long socks with elastic garters to hold them up. I hate garters because they are tight around your legs. I have to keep pulling up my socks when Mum is around or she will know that I'm not wearing garters. Kate wears a dress and short white socks. Dad is in a suit and Mum wears a very smart black dress and a matching black hat.

For children best manners are compulsory. If any of Dad or Mum's friends ask me how I am, I have to smile and say, 'Very well, thank you, Mr Brockhouse' (or whoever it is). I am not allowed to say more than that unless asked.

My father often says, 'Children should be seen and not heard.'

After Church comes Sunday School. This is not so bad but it's not as good as climbing trees, fishing, swimming, exploring drains and doing whatever you feel like. Sunday School is like real school except the teachers are not proper teachers and the classes are smaller and all about Jesus. Today I have been told that Rev Carpenter wants to talk to me after Sunday School. I am nervous about this because sometimes when he looks down from the pulpit he stares straight at me and I'm sure that he can read my mind. I feel as if he knows all about my wicked deeds. Maybe he knows I have been tracing over Blondie's breasts and drawing her in the nude. I give a shiver. I don't want to go. Being faced with such a terrible sin is almost as scary as looking into a grave.

Everyone has gone home and I am alone in the Church Hall with Rev Carpenter. He is the curate. He has big white teeth. They are just as white as the dog collar he wears around his neck. All his clothes are black and so is his thick hair. Blackest of all is his Bible which is large and has little letters and numbers cut into the sides of the pages. He can fan out the sides by bending the book and then he can find the spot of any bit he wants.

The Church Hall is an ancient wooden one which was brought out from England on a sailing ship in the old days. So many people have walked over its floor that the wood has been worn right down. The knots stand up like stones poking out of hard ground. In some places the knots have fallen out and left holes. Cold draughts are blowing in.

Rev Carpenter smiles and shows his big teeth. He is very serious but he's kind.

He puts one hand on my shoulder and stares at me seriously.

'Do you want a new friend, Hedley?' he says.

Wow. I can't believe this. It's not about breasts.

'A faithful friend who will never let you down?' says Rev Carpenter.

My mind is smiling at his words. A faithful friend. Not a rat-bag like Ian Douglas. A boy who will always stand by you. Even when you are called a Pommie.

Rev Carpenter knows I am lonely. He is going to fix me up with a friend who I can play with. I hope this new friend goes to our school.

Fantastic. I won't have to do a dare. I don't really want to join Ian Douglas and his gang. One special friend will be much better than that lot. I nod my head like crazy.

'Yes,' I say happily. 'I really do.'

Rev Carpenter looks pleased. He flips open his Bible.

'Hedley,' he says. 'Read this aloud.'

The page has lots of passages with lines under them. In the margin he has scribbled comments in his own handwriting. I read the passage he is pointing to:

'*All have sinned and come short of the glory of God.*'

'Do you know what that means, Hedley?'

I know that I have to say something or his feelings will be hurt.

'Everyone has done bad things?' I say.

'So that means you,' he says. 'And me.'

Oh what? He knows. He knows about Blondie's breasts. I am dead. This is not working out the way I thought.

'Now read this.' He turns to another page.

'*The wages of sin is death.*'

Rev Carpenter nods slowly and says, 'What does that mean?'

'You get killed for being bad.'

'No, no, no, Hedley. It means eternal death. Being separated from God forever. That is what awaits us. No Heaven. Eternal night. Hell.'

He quickly flips to another verse and this time he reads it out himself.

'*Unless you be born again, you cannot enter the Kingdom of Heaven.*'

'Have you been born again, Hedley?' he says.

'I don't know,' I say. 'I can't even remember the first time.'

Rev Carpenter smiles patiently. 'It means you have to give your heart to Jesus. You have to open the door of your heart and ask him in. Everyone who asks Jesus into their life goes to Heaven. Those who don't, will go to . . .' he doesn't seem to want to say the word '. . . Hell.'

I just look at him. Some questions are stirring in my mind. What about savages and cannibals who can't even read or don't know anything about the Bible? How can they ask Jesus into their heart when they have never heard of him?

I don't say this, though. What do I know? I am just a boy. He is a minister. All the adults sit and listen to him and after the sermon they put money into the collection at Church. He stands out the front and holds out this enormous gold plate. The vestry men (my father is one) take up the collection and then walk out to the altar and put all the money on the gold plate. Rev Carpenter holds it high above his head and offers it to God.

Sometimes I imagine that this gold plate belongs to me. It would be worth millions of pounds for sure. I imagine getting on the bus and I have no money but I have the plate. The bus driver would say, 'Hedley Hopkins, you are the richest person in the country with that plate. You can travel for nothing.' I often have this little daydream. I also have one where I am Superman.

In the Superman daydream I am flying through the sky and everyone points up and says, 'Look, that's Hedley Hopkins. Amazing.'

My favourite daydream is the one where I am walking along the street and a big black car pulls up. A man with a cigar says, 'That's him. That's the kid we need to star in our new picture.'

I go to America with this man and take Mum and Dad and Kate with me. We all become rich and famous because I am a film star like the boy in *Lassie*.

Rev Carpenter brings my mind back to the present. He is very enthusiastic.

'Listen to this, Hedley. This is marvellous. This is wonderful.' He reads from the Bible in a deep voice:

'*Behold I stand at the door and knock. If any*

*man hear my voice and open the door I will come in
to him and sup with him and he with me.'*

Rev Carpenter lays a hand on my shoulder and
looks deeply into my eyes. 'Jesus wants to be your
friend. He is standing at the door of your heart. Will
you ask him in, Hedley?'

I feel embarrassed. I am not going to get a new friend
at school. But I know I can't say 'no' to Rev Carpenter
so I nod.

'Repeat after me,' he says. We both kneel down and
he says a prayer. He stops at the end of each sentence
and I repeat it. A knot in the floor is sticking into my
knee but I don't mention it.

'*Dear Lord Jesus I am a sinner.*'

'Dear Lord Jesus I am a sinner.'

'*Please forgive me and come into my heart.*'

'Please forgive me and come into my heart.'

'*I will be your faithful servant for ever and ever.*'

'I will be your faithful servant for ever and ever.'

'*Amen.*'

'Amen.'

Rev Carpenter springs to his feet with a big smile.
He shakes my hand. 'Congratulations. You now have
eternal life. Wasn't that easy?'

I nod once again. It was embarrassing but it was
easy. He put all the words into my mouth. I just had

to repeat them. Like an echo.

'The next bit is not easy,' he says. 'Now you must go forth and tell others. Never deny that you are a Soldier of Jesus. Win souls for Christ. Tell everyone what you have done. Don't be like Simon Peter who denied Jesus just as the cock crowed.'

I don't say anything. It's okay for Rev Carpenter to tell people about Jesus. But it is not something I want to talk about at school. I have a feeling I will be like Simon Peter and keep my mouth shut.

He nods to the door and I go forth into the sunshine where my parents and Kate are waiting in their Sunday best in our Morris Minor. I can hear the Church choir practising a hymn. The gentle sound floats across the gravel car park.

> What a friend we have in Jesus
> All our sins and griefs to bear.

'What was that about?' says Dad as he puts the car into gear. 'What did he want?'

'Nothing,' I say.

'Did he ask you to sign the Pledge?' says Mum.

'What's that?'

'You have to promise not to drink alcohol for the rest of your life.'

I think about this. I've had a couple of sips of Mum's

sherry and it is awful. Dad's beer is even worse. I just don't want anyone to know about me being a Soldier of Jesus so I say, 'Yes, I signed the Pledge.'

Mum seems glad. Dad seems sad. He likes his glass of beer on a hot day. For a moment I wonder if one day he would like me to have one with him. But he doesn't say anything.

It's funny – I'm in the car with three other people but I still feel lonely. As we drive down the street my mind starts to wander. Maybe I could trace over Betty in the *Archie* comics.

I wonder what she would look like in the nude?

5

the dare

THE NEXT DAY I drift around the playground at lunch-time like the first autumn leaf blowing across Hyde Park back home in England. I need someone to talk to. Kate is in the girls' part of the playground jumping a skipping rope with two other girls. But even if she wasn't I couldn't be seen playing with my little sister.

I am not quite sure why I don't have any friends of my own age. Is it just because I am a Pommie? I'm working on talking like the other kids at school. I can already say 'G'day' and 'How'ya goin', mate?' Some-times I say 'Fair dinkum?' but not often. My mother says I am starting to sound common.

Common people include ladies who wear earrings and paint their toenails. Boys who swear and have dirt under their fingernails are also common. I like common people – they are interesting. Mum says the Dunny Man is common. He comes once a week to collect the poo from the outside toilet. He heaves our enormous can of filthy poop and pee on to one shoulder and takes it out to his horse and cart in the street.

Every boy in the school has a story about the Dunny Man tripping up and sending the contents of the stinking pan flying all over the lawn. I have never seen this happen and I do not believe it. Ian Douglas boasts that he once tripped the Dunny Man up but no one believes this either.

The Dunny Man fought in the War. If your father fought in the War you get to wear his medals on Anzac Day at school when we remember the dead soldiers. If your father did not fight in the War it's not as good as if he did. My father did not. He was the foreman of a factory that made aeroplanes in England. So I don't get to wear any medals but I wish I did.

The Dunny Man sometimes sings rude songs from his days in the army. One of them makes me laugh and the boys at school sing it when there are no teachers around. I know it off by heart.

Hitler has only one brass ball.
Rommel has two but they are small.
Himmler has something similar.
But poor old Goebbels has no balls at all.

Other common people are those who do not speak English. Our street has a lot of people from Greece, Italy, Yugoslavia and Poland. My mother calls them 'foreigners'.

'They're always kissing each other,' she says. 'And they eat garlic. You can smell it on them for days.'

In our family we do not kiss each other. I can't remember ever having been hugged by my father or mother. English people do not show how they feel. And they do not eat garlic. We have roast beef with Yorkshire pudding, gravy and boiled vegetables.

'We are foreigners, too,' I said one day.

'No,' said Dad in a cross voice. 'The foreigners don't even speak the Queen's English. They come out here for the jobs. They don't belong to the British Empire. What do you see in the Australian flag? Our flag, the Union Jack, that's what. If you are English, you are Australian as soon as you put your foot on the shore.'

But this is not what the children here think. Over here I am a misfit.

I have to take action.

I have to make something happen so that I have friends.

Ian Douglas and his friends are in the boys' toilets. They are probably smoking. Everyone knows they smoke in the toilets. Even the teachers know. But no one can catch them. They have a lookout on the door. It is usually Mouse because he gets asthma and can't smoke. That's what he says anyway. The others sit on the toilets with their trousers down and cigarettes dangling out of their mouths. If a teacher comes, Mouse shouts out and all the gang members drop their cigarettes between their legs and flush the toilets quicker than you can blink. All that is left is a bit of smoke drifting around and no one can say where it came from.

The teachers could sniff the breath of the gang members if they wanted to but for some reason they never do. To be perfectly honest I don't blame them. I wouldn't sniff Ian Douglas's breath. Not for all the tea in China.

I don't really like these boys much although Mouse is probably all right. He is only little. His dare was to blow up Mr Cordingly's letterbox with a handful of penny bangers. He got caught and taken to the Police Station. The whole school knew about it because he had to apologise in front of everyone. Ian Douglas had to let him join the gang because he did the dare. That is the rule.

I go into the toilets to talk to Ian Douglas. I feel sick. It is not because the boys' toilets stink of pee – which they do. It is because I am putting so much effort into looking normal and trying not to shake like a jelly. Ian Douglas takes a puff of his cigarette and looks up.

'Look who's here,' he says in a sarcastic voice. 'Whadda ya want, Hopkins? Come in for a bog, have ya?'

'Well, a little turd like him would, wouldn't 'e?' says Henderson who is sitting in the next cubicle with the door open.

'I want to be one of your gang,' I say quickly.

'Do you hear that, Kelly?' says Ian Douglas. 'Hopkins wants to hang out with us.'

Frank Kelly has his back to us. He is seeing how high he can pee up the urinal. He can almost reach the window.

'Piss weak,' says Henderson. 'Just like little Hopkins.'

'Let's see you do better, Henderson,' says Kelly. 'You couldn't hit your own boot.'

'Now, now, boys,' says Ian Douglas. 'What're we gonna do about little Hopkins 'ere? I think we should give him a chance. He might have enough guts.'

'Never,' says Henderson.

They are talking about me as if I am not there. I search around for words that will make me sound tough.

'I bloody do have guts,' I say.

I can't believe that I just said this swear word.

'We don't like bloody Pommies,' says Henderson.

'Why not?'

'Because they're whingers,' says Frank Kelly.

I feel like running away. You just can't win with these boys. But somewhere inside I find a bit of courage.

'What about the Queen?' I say.

This has got them. Four years ago the King died. I came down to breakfast one morning and my parents were sad. They had the wireless on and every station was playing funeral music. There was no *Air Adventures of Biggles*. Every hour the music would stop and the man reading the news would tell everyone in England and the Commonwealth what had happened. He would finish by saying, 'The King is dead. Long live the Queen.'

The Queen is young and beautiful. She is going to come to Australia this year and everyone loves her. No one can say anything against the Queen. I once asked my mother if the Queen went to the toilet.

She laughed and said, 'Of course she does.'

But I just can't see it. I can imagine her sitting on her white horse and reviewing the troops. But not sitting on the toilet.

'You're not the Queen, Hopkins,' says Henderson. 'We don't want ya.'

'Don't be too hasty,' says Ian Douglas. 'Let him prove himself.'

'He's a scaredy-cat,' says Henderson.

Mouse has wandered inside and is listening. 'Give him a chance,' he says. 'Hopkins isn't a bad kid.'

I give Mouse a weak smile. He is all right. But Henderson is really mean. I remember the day I saw him and some other boys playing jacks on the pavement after school. Jacks are small bones that come out of lamb shanks. You throw them up and catch them on the back of your hand. When you first get them out of a leg of lamb the knuckle bones have gristle on them. The only way to get it off is to put the bones on a bull ants' nest and let them chew it off. The bull ants go crazy when they get anywhere near a bone. You can also buy plastic jacks but they are not as good.

'Can I join in?' I said to Henderson and the others.

'Well, Pommie Hopkins, where're ya jacks?' said Henderson.

'At home.'

32

'Well, ya can't play without 'em, can ya?' he said in a scornful voice.

I walked all the way home. It was a long way but I fetched my jacks and walked back again.

'Henderson, I've got my jacks,' I said. I held them out to show him.

'They're plastic,' he said. 'We only use the real thing.'

In my heart I knew that even if I had gold-plated jacks, Henderson would never have let me join in. Now he doesn't want me around as usual but Ian Douglas is showing interest.

'Will you do a dare?' he says.

'What is it?' I ask.

He looks at me as if I'm stupid.

'You really are a spastic,' says Henderson.

Frank Kelly is shaking his head as if I am an idiot.

I *am* an idiot. What am I doing here?

Ian Douglas looks straight into my eyes with a mocking grin. 'Ya don't get to know what ya have to do until you've agreed to do it. That's what it's all about.'

This is one of those moments where a wave of fate changes your life forever. If I say 'yes', I will have to go through with it. If I say 'no', I will go back to being a Pommie autumn leaf blowing around on the bare ground.

I think about it for about thirty seconds. It seems more like thirty minutes. Finally I take a deep breath.

'All right,' I say in my toughest voice. 'I will do the bloody dare.'

'Impressive,' says Ian Douglas. He drops his cigarette butt into the toilet and flushes it away. Then he pulls up his trousers. This is the signal for Henderson to do the same.

We all walk outside into the sunshine and he begins to tell me what I knew he would. This dark thought that has been trying to get out of my mind now comes to life.

'Okay, Hopkins,' says Ian Douglas. 'Here's what ya have to do. Behind the Loony Bin in the sand dunes there's a grave. Someone's pulled the top off . . .'

'And busted into the coffin,' yells Frank Kelly.

Ian Douglas gives him a dirty look. 'I'm telling this,' he says.

Frank Kelly shuts up.

'Someone's taken the skull outta the coffin and left it in the grave,' says Ian Douglas. 'You have to go there. Tonight. After dark. You have to climb down into the hole and get the skull. Then you have to bring it back to me.'

My brain is numb. It's sort of like when a teacher asks you a question and your mind goes blank. I hear

Ian Douglas talking but the words don't mean anything. I blink and shake my head.

'That, Hedley Hopkins, is your dare,' Ian Douglas finishes.

The world spins around me. I feel faint. They want me to touch the skull. It is not a plastic thing like you see in toy shops. It is not a joke like on cartoons at the pictures. It is not even a dancing made-up skeleton. It is the head of a real person. A dead person. And they want me to pick it up.

Frank Kelly starts to laugh. 'It's still got some hair on it,' he hoots. 'And skin.'

Ian Douglas throws him another dirty look. The gang seems to know a lot about this skull. I think I know who has broken open the grave but I don't mention it.

'I have to go to the Father and Son Night with my dad,' I say in a soft voice.

'That's right,' says Mouse. 'I'm going too.'

'Sneak out afterwards,' says Frank Kelly. 'After ya get home. When your old man's asleep.'

'How do I get into the grave?' I say. 'It's deep.'

'You'll need a ladder, idiot,' says Ian Douglas. 'There's one hidden under the old pier. You can use that.'

My mouth starts to move. I can't believe what I am about to say. What is wrong with me? Why am I speaking these words?

'No bloody worries,' I say, trying to put on an Australian accent.

'Hey, I just thought of something,' says Henderson.

'What?' says Ian Douglas.

'When Hedley Hopkins takes the skull, the skeleton will be headless.'

'So?'

'So. Headless Hopkins. Get it?'

They all start to laugh. I try to look as if I don't care. But I do. *Headless* is a bit like *brainless*. I don't like it.

'Good one,' says Ian Douglas.

The school bell goes and we all begin to walk inside.

'I won't be able to see in the dark,' I say. 'I don't have a torch.'

'*I don't have a torch*,' mimics Ian Douglas. 'So what? There's a full moon tonight.' He gives a long, long laugh. 'You know that Loonies bury people alive when the moon is out. But you won't have to worry about that. I'm sure they like Pommies.'

'For breakfast, Headless,' says Henderson.

I suddenly go cold all over and start to shiver.

6

the facts of life

THE FATHER and Son Night is about the facts of life. It is a topic I am interested in and I want to know more. But I don't really want to go to this meeting with my father.

Dad and I walk towards the old Church Hall under the full moon. As I go I think about the skull. I am not going to do it. I just can't touch a dead person's head. And the grave is right next to the Loony Bin. I feel sick at the thought of it. I will just have to go on being lonely. That is all.

Sometimes I think my father is lonely too. When we first arrived in Australia, my father couldn't find work. He was finally offered a job on an ice truck. The iceman brings a huge hunk of ice to every house in the street and puts it inside people's ice chests. An ice chest keeps the food cool and stops the blowflies getting to it.

Dad would not take the job.

'I am an engineer,' he said. 'Not a labourer. And anyway, everyone will have fridges one day. All the ice chests will be down the dump and I will be out of work.'

We all laughed at this.

'Only rich people have fridges,' said Mum.

She was wrong about this. My father finally got a job as foreman in a factory that makes fridges. They let him buy a fridge cheap because he works there. We were the first ones in our street to get one.

Our fridge has a freezing compartment inside at the top which you can use to make ice-cream. Homemade ice-cream is not as good as a brick of the real thing which you buy wrapped in a cardboard box from the milk bar. Homemade ice-cream has flakes of ice in it but bought ice-cream is smooth.

When we came out from England on the boat, I thought Australia was going to be full of kangaroos, frill-necked lizards, snakes, stockmen on horses and Aborigines dancing around camp fires. I haven't seen any of these things yet. Everything is the same as in England except for the roads which are not sealed and are filled with puddles in the winter. And the way people talk. And football. Cricket is the same, but everyone follows Australia so I have to as well or the others will tease me if England loses.

Tonight as we walk the dark streets my father is quiet, which is unusual. Mostly he is a talker. Whenever we are at the table having dinner he says much more than anyone else. He likes to tell stories about funny things that have happened. Some of the stories teach you lessons like: 'Save your money and work hard and you will get ahead like me.' I have heard every story hundreds of times but still he keeps on telling them.

'Er, you already told us that one, Dad,' I will say.

He doesn't even hear. He just tells the whole thing over again. This is why Kate and I never ask him anything. He just can't stop giving advice and telling stories. I hate these stories but for some reason I can't show my feelings and stop him doing it. If I did, it would be like hitting him. If I stand up to him, he will shatter into a million pieces like a glass ornament.

No one can stop him talking once he gets going.

On the subject of the Facts of Life my father has nothing to say. We walk in silence.

Earlier Mum had said, 'Your dad is taking you to a Father and Son Night.'

When I asked what it was about she said, 'You'll find out.'

Dad just nodded. I could tell he didn't want to go.

I know that it is about the Facts of Life because Ian Douglas and his gang were going on about it all day. They were making rude jokes about it.

Finally Dad and I reach the Church Hall. We walk inside and sit down on a long wooden pew. A lot of the boys from my school are there. Others I have never seen before. They are all sitting next to their fathers. No one is talking. Everyone looks embarrassed.

Mr Hooper is there too. He is a teacher from the school inside the Loony Bin. Sometimes he comes and fills in at our school when a teacher is away. He has a wide face, dark hair and a flat nose. He smiles a lot and he seems to like me for some reason. I wish he was my teacher because he is kind and doesn't give the strap to boys who misbehave. He is sitting next to a weird-looking kid. This boy is bigger than all the rest of us. He has a bald head and no eyebrows. His eyes are narrow and he keeps making laughing noises. Mr Hooper touches him gently on the arm.

'Not now, Victor,' he says in a kind voice.

Once, when I mentioned Mr Hooper at home, my father said, 'I think he has a touch of the tar brush.'

Tar is black sticky stuff they put on the asphalt

roads. When I asked what Dad meant my mother said, 'Don't talk like that, Albert.' I never did find out.

The bald boy stares at me. I stare back.

'Don't encourage him,' whispers Dad. 'He's a Mongol.'

I am just about to ask what that is when Rev Carpenter comes out the front and tells us that he is glad we have come. He pins up a lot of charts and pictures on a board at the front. He tells us that The Lord wants us to know how to love each other properly.

I look up at the ceiling which is made out of floorboards. There are five hundred and twenty-two boards in the ceiling. I know this because I count them during Sunday School when it is boring, which it nearly always is. Tonight I do not count the boards because Rev Carpenter begins talking about babies and where they come from. This is what the meeting is really about. He points to different bits of the charts which are mainly of men and women sliced down the middle so you can see inside them. There are tubes and things running everywhere. I can't quite figure out what all this has to do with The Lord.

He works through all the bits about where babies grow and how they come out. I already know this part. But there is one bit I do not know. I can't work out how the babies get started. I have heard stories in the playground but which ones are true?

No adult has ever spoken about them.

My suspicions are shown to be right about how babies get started. You have to put your stiffy into the lady and pee into her. That's how it seems to me from all the diagrams anyway. Rev Carpenter doesn't seem to want to actually say it out loud. Dad is looking at the ceiling. Don't tell me he is counting the boards up there. No, I think he's looking at a fly.

Just as it seems as if the talk is coming to an end, Rev Carpenter says, 'Boys, we must always have clean minds. When I say this some of you will be thinking: "Last night I had bad thoughts".'

'Last night I had bad thoughts,' yells Victor.

Everyone is embarrassed. 'Thank you, Victor,' says Rev Carpenter. To the rest of us he says, 'Victor is from Billabong.'

'Victor is from Billabong,' says Victor.

Billabong. My blood freezes. That's the name of the Loony Bin. Victor is crazy. He is a loony. He could be a murderer if the moon was out. Which it is.

Mr Hooper gently pulls Victor down into his seat.

Much more is said about bad thoughts. According to Rev Carpenter, these come from the Devil who puts them into our heads. Even *thinking* something bad is as wicked as actually doing it. He says that as the Devil's voice is loud we can drown out the bad thoughts about women by running around the block and taking a cold shower before going to bed.

He goes on for a bit more on this subject and then at last it is all over. Or nearly all over. Rev Carpenter passes out small pieces of paper and pencils. 'If you have any questions write them down,' he says. 'I will read them out. No one will know who has asked the questions. That way no one need be embarrassed.'

I take my piece of paper and write out a question. This is my chance to find out the bit I don't understand about the whole thing. I fold the paper twenty times so that no one can read it.

'Pass your questions along to the end of the row,' says Rev Carpenter. I give mine to Dad and he passes it on. He looks worried.

Suddenly my heart goes cold.

I can't believe what I am seeing.

No, no, no. It can't be true. Give it back. Give it back.

Too late.

Mine is the only piece of paper that is moving. No one else has asked a question. Everyone will know that the question is mine. Rev Carpenter takes the paper and beams at me with his toothy smile.

'You don't mind if I read it out, do you, Hedley?' he says.

Before I can open my mouth which has already frozen with fear, he reads the question. He has betrayed me. Everyone knows it was me who asked this. The words I have written seem frozen in the air for all time.

'How much pee do you put in?'

Well. The whole hall bursts into laughter. Oh, shame. Oh, horror. The fathers laugh. The boys laugh. Even Rev Carpenter laughs. My own father goes red. I can see he is ashamed of me. The loudest laughs of all come from Ian Douglas and his mates. They go on and on and on.

What have I said?

What? What? What?

Oh, I can't stand it. The boards in the roof and the knot holes in the floor and the Cubs' banner on the wall seem to laugh. I jump to my feet and run for the door. I have to get away from that laughter. I am dumb. I am the dumbest person in the world. I don't know anything. *I* should be in the Loony Bin.

My legs, like they always do, want to carry me away to a safe place. The laughing faces line my route. I am an alien. I have landed in a world where everyone knows the rules except me.

I am a freak.

An outsider.

7

a silent scream

I FLEE INTO the black night outside. I can hear Rev Carpenter's voice calling out my name. He wants me to go back. He is sorry that they all laughed.

He might be sorry – but not as sorry as I am going to be. Tomorrow at school it will go around. Whatever it was that I said that was stupid.

I run and run and run until my breath cuts into my lungs like a saw. You can't get away from things like shame and guilt because they are inside you. But for some reason the running makes you feel that you are escaping. In the end I have to stop and the embarrassment of the Father and Son Night catches up with me.

My face is burning in the light of the full moon.

I am at the beach. There is no one around. I shiver. I left my coat behind in the hall. I bend over and suck in the cold night air with shuddering gasps. The empty sea shimmers. The only sound is the roar of the crashing waves.

I still don't know what was so funny. Victor the mad kid was laughing like crazy. He was looking from face to face not knowing what was going on but laughing even though he didn't get it. Oh, I will never live this down. I will be a joke. I am a joke. What can I do? How can I stop the whole school laughing at me?

There is only one thing for it. The skull. If I turn up at school with a real live skull no one will mock me. Everyone will be amazed. This is the biggest dare ever.

I will do it.

I will go to the grave and get the skull.

Even if it means jail. Or worse.

The sand is soft under my feet. The full moon shimmers on the ocean making a silvery ladder.

Ladder.

Somewhere under the pier is a ladder that I can use to get down into the grave. The pier is high above the sand where it touches the water but as it runs back into the sloping beach the space beneath gets smaller and smaller. I can't see a ladder anywhere so I lie down on my stomach and wiggle forward beneath the planks at the low end. Yes, there is something there. I grasp the end of a long pole and push myself backwards, pulling it out with me.

It's not much of a ladder. Just one long length of timber with bits of driftwood nailed across for rungs. I can tell already that it won't be easy climbing up and down it because it's going to wobble from side to side.

I start the long walk along the beach to the grave. The ladder is heavy so I drag it behind me. The end makes a long trail in the sand. It looks like the track of a giant snake.

The sounds of the waves roar loudly. No one would hear me if I called out. The beach is as empty as the full moon so far above.

Finally, after about an hour or so, I reach the place where the track leads up through the sand dunes towards the grave. It is hard work pulling the ladder up the steep sand but somehow I manage to get to the top. I can see the big wire fence of the Loony Bin. No one could climb over it. Or under it, because it is fixed into a ribbon of concrete at the bottom.

Then I see something which sends a chill through my bones.

A hole. A hole in the wire fence.

Someone has cut a hole big enough to climb through the Loony Bin fence.

I try to tell myself that someone has been breaking in.

But deep inside I know they could have been breaking out.

I must go on. I turn my attention to the grave. There it is. The concrete slab is still off to one side. The grave is still open. This time the black hole makes me think of the entrance to the Underworld. I have heard creepy things like that on my crystal set when I am supposed to be asleep. Hell would start at a grave.

I was crazy agreeing to do the dare.

My stomach feels like there is a live jellyfish in there trying to get out. I just want to turn and run. But I don't. I lower the ladder down the open grave until it touches the bottom near the end of the coffin. I nervously put my foot over the edge and feel around for the top rung.

I find it and put my weight on to it. The whole thing starts to wobble wildly and the top of the ladder suddenly slides to one side. *Whap*. It hits the edge of the grave and my feet lose their hold. I cling to the top rung desperately. My legs flail in the air. The rung snaps with a loud crack and I plunge down. I land heavily on my side next to the coffin.

I don't scream out loud because I can't. I have no air. So I scream silently at the bony face lying next to my own. I am looking straight into the vacant eyes of the skull. It leers at me. I fight for breath but I am totally winded.

The skull has a large hole at the back. And on the top is a tiny patch of skin with a few hairs growing out of it. It is this hair that makes it so terrible. Wild visions run through my mind like scenes from a nightmare. Once this skull belonged to a man who combed his hair and had soft lips. And now it has all gone – shrivelled and eaten by worms. I know that I will never be able to touch the bony remains. Never in a million years.

The face seems to warp and scowl just a few inches from my nose.

Suddenly there is something worse. Is this a nightmare? Oh, please let me wake up and be home in bed. No, no, it is true. The terrible sight is real. Above me at the top of the grave is another horrible face.

But this one is alive. His bald head shines in the moonlight like a dancing white bowling ball. He bobs about, skipping from side to side. His laugh echoes loudly and seems to bounce off the moon itself. He begins jumping from side to side like a monkey and pelting me with small hard missiles. He sends handful after handful raining down onto my head.

It is Victor – the loony.

Now there are more loonies. Five or six. A couple of them have bald heads and one has no teeth. Some of their faces have a lot of wrinkles. Too many for their age. And some have almond-shaped eyes. One of them has a huge head. I didn't know that it was possible to have such a big head. They are all laughing crazily like Victor did in the Father and Son Night. The whole lot of them begin throwing down more hard pellets. I am trapped. There is no way out except up the ladder, straight into their arms.

'Stop,' I shriek. 'Leave me alone. Go away.'

The sound of my voice only makes them worse. And the pellets rain down even heavier. I have always been scared of crazy people. Not that I have ever met any. But I have read about them in comics and there are stories. You can't reason with them. And this lot are crazy, the whole lot of them. My heart is beating as if a million hammers are knocking on my ribs.

Instinctively, I look around for something to throw back. I have to stop this storm from above. It is defend myself or die.

Grab me, the skull seems to say.

In my terror I grab the skull and heave it with all my might. It arcs up towards the moon and then begins to fall. Victor catches it like a goalkeeper and then stares down in amazement at his prize. He shrieks with the cry of an enraged wolf and throws it to the crazy guy next to him. They all start howling and screaming. Then their heads disappear.

I am alone in the grave except for the headless skeleton inside the lead coffin.

I take a deep breath and try to make my brain slow down. I have to get out of this terrible hole. But what will I find above? Are they lying in wait? Have they gone to get more loonies? The thought fills me with even more horror. I begin to climb frantically up the ladder but it starts to wobble again. One rung is missing and I can't find where to put my foot. If I fall back down again I could break a leg or worse.

But I don't.

I manage to heave myself up the wobbling ladder into the cold night.

There on the edge of the grave is the skull.

Victor has dropped it.

From somewhere inside myself I find a tiny grain of courage. I pull a handkerchief out of my pocket and lift the skull by the little bridge between the eye sockets. I take care not to let my fingers touch it. I take one deep breath and lurch off towards the water.

8

R.I.P.

THE NIGHT IS cold now and mist from the pounding waves makes my shirt and pants damp. I would walk closer to the sand dunes but I want to stay out in the open where no one can jump out and get me. I keep throwing a look over my shoulder to make sure the loonies are not on my tail.

I try not to stare down at what is in my hand. This skull makes my flesh crawl.

Suddenly a nasty thought comes into my head. What if this person died of some terrible disease? In the old days they had illnesses like Leprosy and the Black Death. What if there are germs hiding under that bit of flesh? Or in the hairs that are still attached to it? I put the skull down on the sand and start to scratch. I feel itchy all over.

Put me in a box, the skull seems to say.

I stare around at where the seaweed is drying out at the high-water mark. This is where stuff that is washed up is to be found. I've often looked among the sea-weed hoping to find treasure or a message in a bottle. Wouldn't it be great if there was a message from my granny back in England? Inside the bottle would be a thousand pounds. Enough money for us all to go back to England to live. I could go to my old school again where everyone has the same accent as me.

But there is no bottle with money in it. All I see are things like a twisted piece of rope, an old sandal, a dead fish, bits of white wood that have been roughly rounded by sand and rubbish such as mouldy potatoes thrown off ships.

Then I see something different. I find some treasure. Well, it's treasure to me. An old sack half-buried in the sand.

I pull the sack out, and still holding the skull gently with my handkerchief, drop it into the sack. Now I won't have to touch it. I won't even have to look at it.

The skull is out of sight but it is not out of mind. I start to feel guilty. One day after I am dead my own head will be in a grave somewhere. The thought of someone walking along the beach with it in a sack fills me with guilt. I know I wouldn't like it if I was dead. The skull seems to weigh a ton. It's heavy in my hand and it's heavy on my mind.

The dead should rest in peace. R.I.P. – Rest In Peace – that's what it means. But I am a grave robber and this man is resting in pieces. All his parts should be together. I have made off with this skull just so I can make friends at school and save myself from looking stupid over the pee.

I start to wonder who this man was. I think he must have been famous or important. I wonder what his name is. I should apologise to him.

A song comes into my mind. A song we had to learn on Anzac Day at school. A hymn that remembers the soldiers who died in the War:

> We will remember them today,
> Who from their homeland sailed away.
> So bravely and so willingly,
> To give their lives for you and me.
> Father, guard their sleeping.

Whenever I think of this song I try hard not to let tears come into my eyes. I think of those men going off to war and not coming back.

Back in England, my granny has a faded picture

of my grandfather in his World War One uniform. He was young and smiling, not knowing that he was going to die in a trench from an enemy bullet. Granny has grown old and wrinkled. She never married again after Grandad died. She says he was the love of her life. His young face smiles at her old one every day from its place in a frame next to her bed. Sometimes I used to wonder what he would think if he came back from Heaven and found her all wrinkled while he was not. He would still love her. I do.

What if the skull belonged to a soldier like my grandfather? A brave man who fought for his country? I might have taken the skull from a sacred grave. A war memorial. Like The Unknown Soldier at the Shrine in Melbourne. No one knows who he was.

'I'm sorry, Major Manners,' I say in a sad voice. 'I didn't want to disturb your sleeping. But I had no choice. The boys at school are picking on me.'

I don't know where I got that name from except that on the grave is part of a word. I remember it said MANN. *Major Manners* just sort of popped into my head. Something inside of me says that this man was a soldier. A warrior.

'I am really, really, really sorry,' I say again.

It's okay, cobber, says Major Manners. *You'll put me to rest when the time comes. I trust you.*

The skull does not actually say this in words that you can hear. It just talks to me inside my head. It makes me feel better. I walk all the rest of the way home without looking back over my shoulder. Major Manners has given me a little bit of his courage.

9

worth your weight in sawdust

WHEN I GET back the house is in darkness except for the sitting room. It is all lit up. I peer through the window and see Mum darning a sock. She is sitting in front of the electric fire. It is one of those fires with a red light bulb that shines beneath painted metal coals. The heat from the light turns a tiny fan which throws flickering shadows on to Mum's worried face. The fire is a fake. It is like our teacher, Mr Tinker, who is different on the outside to what he really is on the inside.

No one likes Mr Tinker because he is a bully and he gives the boys the strap at the slightest excuse. This is the reason we all change his name from Tinker to Stinker when he is not there. For some reason he seems to hate me. He will give me the strap for the smallest mistake. Even things I can't help, like getting a sum wrong.

My father says that if you get a punishment at school you should get another dose of the same thing when you get home. This is why I never complain about what Stinker does. I can see my father through the window now, standing looking at himself in the mantelpiece mirror. He stands stiffly like he always does when there is a problem.

Once I saw a man standing on the end of the pier watching the sunset. He was just a black silhouette against the red sky.

'There's Dad,' I said to Mum.

'That's not your father,' she said. 'He would never stand like that.'

I knew straightaway that she was right. The man was standing with one foot up on a bench with his elbow on his knee. He was leaning against his fist in a really relaxed way. Like a male model getting their photo taken for an advert for jumpers or cardigans. Even when he wasn't posing for a photo, my father always stood like someone getting their portrait taken in the olden days.

Straight up, with an embarrassed look on his face. Trying to smile but not being able to do it.

On another occasion Mum said, 'He is uncomfortable in his skin.'

I am not sure what that means but it makes me remember the little bit of skin on Major Manners' head. I cannot waltz into the house with a skull in a sack. I have to hide it.

I walk round to the back garden and push the sack in behind a shiny-leaf bush. 'I'm going to leave you here for a while,' I say. 'But I'll be back. You can count on me, Sir.'

No worries, says Major Manners.

A feeling of dread fills my heart as I walk slowly across the dark lawn towards the back door. In books kids run away and join the circus and become rich and go back home in triumph. But in real life you just have to crawl back with your tail between your legs because you have no money and you don't meet anyone and there is nowhere to sleep. I am going to be in big trouble for running away and staying out late at night. I know I am.

I will just have to go in with a stiff upper lip. Like Biggles who is a pilot in my favourite book. He is fearless in every situation.

When I step in the door of the sitting room, Mum's face lights up with a happy smile. But just for a second.

The smile vanishes quicker than one of Ian Douglas's cigarette butts disappearing down the toilet.

'What are you thinking of, Hedley?' Mum yells. 'We have been sick to death with worry. Where have you been, you thoughtless child?'

My shoes are covered in sand. I have to tell the truth.

'The beach,' I mumble.

'Why did you run off?' she asks.

I look at Dad. He didn't tell her about my stupid question at the Father and Son Night.

My father's not brave. One day I found a little sliding bolt on the inside of my parents' bedroom door.

'What did you put that there for?' I asked.

Dad looked nervously at Mum. Then he said, 'In case burglars come in the night.'

I didn't say anything, but I thought, 'You coward. Kate and I will be left out with the burglar while you are safe behind a locked door.' I was very disappointed with my father.

But now it is my parents' turn to be disappointed in me.

'You are an ungrateful child, Hedley Hopkins,' says Mum. 'Get out of my sight. Go to bed. You're more trouble than you are worth. You're good for nothing.'

'Not worth your weight in sawdust,' says my father.

Whenever they are mad at me they say I am good for nothing. It is true. I am not really good at anything. I can't play sport. I can't do sums properly. And I don't have any friends because I have an English accent. The only things I am good at are running away and imagining things inside my head and these don't count.

I go into my room and shut the door. I look out of the window down to the shiny-leaf bush at the bottom of the garden.

'Goodnight, Major Manners, Sir.' I say.

Goodnight, mate, he replies. *Take it easy. You're a good bloke.*

10

the first sign of madness

NEXT MORNING I wake early and open my eyes to a feeling of dread. At first I am not sure where I am or what has happened. I am not even sure who I am. I often feel like this when I first open my eyes. It is as if the world has all just been made and I am trying to figure it out for the first time. Slowly, bits of memories come back like ink seeping along a piece of blotting paper. Now the feeling of dread has turned itself into memories.

I remember the Father and Son Night and everyone laughing at me. I remember that I am going to have to face up to Ian Douglas and his gang. They will make mean jokes about me because I asked the question,

'How much pee do you put in?' I must be the only boy in the world who does not know. Everyone else knows how much.

I just lie there staring at the ceiling.

Suddenly I grin.

I have the skull.

Yes, I imagine the look on everyone's face when they see me with the skull. I can smuggle it to school with me and show the gang.

I have passed the test.

No one has ever done anything as brave as this before. They will be amazed. Shocked out of their brains. I might even end up leader of the gang.

I jump out of bed, have a shower and get dressed. I pull on my short pants and long socks but don't wear garters. I put on my leather boots and a jumper because it is cold.

Mum doesn't like the leather school boots. She says they are what the 'working class' boys wear and she prefers shoes because we are 'middle class'. But for once I manage to talk her into it because every other boy in the class wears boots.

At breakfast I can see that Kate still wants to tell everything about the grave. It is not that she is scared – it's just that she still thinks it's the right thing to do. She looks at me with big round eyes. She does not know that I have the skull but she knows about the grave. I shake my head at her and make my eyes big and round like hers. She takes a breath to talk but then closes her mouth. Kate and I understand each other. We can almost read each other's minds.

My father cannot read our minds but he is reading something out from the paper. It is about vandals who glued a beer bottle into the hand of a statue of Queen Victoria. They broke the other hand off and threw red paint over her head.

Queen Victoria has been dead for ages but Dad still likes her.

'She didn't like drunks or fools,' said Dad. 'Like the vandals who did this.'

'What's a vandal?' asks Kate.

I wish she had not asked this question. I have heard the answer before. Dad goes into a long explanation about the Roman Empire in all its glory which was not as good as the British Empire but still impressive. The first Vandals were wild people who attacked Rome and broke everything that was beautiful. He finishes up with, 'Vandals destroy what they can't understand.'

I know that I will be called a vandal if I am caught with Major Manners. Everyone will say I broke into the coffin and stole the skull. But I am not a vandal. Major Manners talks to me in my mind. I understand about the sad soldiers like him who died in the War and stopped the invaders. I understand what it must be like inside a lonely grave. It is like the inside of my head.

'They should be locked up,' says my mother. 'There's no respect for anything any more.'

Dad nods. 'Yes. Whoever did it should be horse-whipped.'

This is his favourite saying about someone who has committed a crime or done a foul deed. *They should be horsewhipped*. I should be horsewhipped because I have stolen Major Manners from the grave. I know this is what the adults will think. I personally do not think that anyone should be horsewhipped. I don't think horses should be horsewhipped for that matter. The Dunny Man never whips his horse. He just yells, 'Cargo loaded, Mabel,' and the horse walks on. Then he yells, 'Whoa, Mabel,' and the horse stops at the next house.

It is a sunny but cold winter day so I do up the buttons on my overcoat and sneak into the back garden. As I go I pass the chopping block next to our chicken run where seven chickens and a rooster walk around scratching all day. The rooster is king over the chickens which we keep for eggs. Over here chickens are called chooks. Dad kills a chicken at

Christmas or for some other special occasion. I have to help him. It is my job to hold the chook by its legs and put its neck on the chopping block. The chicken does not like this and it tries to peck me. It flaps its wings like a tornado. *Whack*. The axe comes down and the chicken loses its head. I let go of the legs and the chicken runs around the back garden like crazy. With no head. This is true. Most of the children at school say their chooks run around after their heads have been chopped off.

I do not like seeing the chook's head on the ground. Removing a head from a body is not right. In my heart I know this.

I walk down to the bottom of the garden where the sack is still hidden in the shiny-leaf bush. I lift up the end of the sack and peer inside. Major Manners is still there. I will try him out on a question.

'How much pee do you put in to make a baby?' I suddenly ask out loud.

Maybe it's not pee, he says. *Maybe it's something else.*

'Like what?'

Think about it, he says.

Right then I hear Mum's voice. She is coming up behind me.

'Hedley, who are you talking to?'

My heart seems to stop. I quickly shove the skull back into the bush.

I say the first thing that comes into my mind. 'No one.'

She shakes her head.

'You are a strange boy. Talking to yourself is the first sign of madness, you know. Quickly now. You'll be late for school.'

I don't move. I need to take the sack but Mum will want to know what's in it for sure.

'Now.'

'Hurry up, Hedley,' yells Kate from the front gate. 'We're going to be late for school.'

'All right, all right,' I yell back. 'Keep your shirt on.' Mum watches me go. Oh, this is terrible. I am walking to school without the skull. When I get there I will be a fool – not a hero. No one will believe I've got the skull. I am really going to cop it.

Kate and I hurry along the path with our satchels on our backs. Kate is counting her swap cards which are the big craze at school. She has a great collection including a lot featuring horses. All the girls want the cards with horses. A boy would not be seen dead with swap cards. Marbles and jacks are the craze at the moment. So is British Bulldog which is a very rough running game where you are lifted off the ground if you are caught by the boys chasing you.

'We should have told Mum,' says Kate. 'About the grave and someone taking the skull out of the coffin. She could call the Police.'

'No, no, no,' I say. 'Don't even think about it. We'll get into terrible trouble just for going there.' I pause for a second and then I say something really crafty. 'And anyway, they might think *we* did it.'

Kate is shocked at this suggestion. 'We couldn't climb down that big, deep hole. Ugh,' she says. 'Only a loony would touch a skull. Children couldn't go down into a grave.'

'The Police don't know that we couldn't get down,' I say. 'There was a ladder.'

'No there wasn't,' says Kate.

'I saw one in the grass,' I say. That was a lie and I feel bad about it so I turn my mind to other things. I think about school. When I get there I am going to be teased terribly. Without the skull I am just a fool. Like the kids in Billabong.

'I *am* mad,' I say under my breath. 'Talking to myself again.'

11

the drum cupboard

WHEN WE GET to school, Kate runs off to the girls'
playground. The gang are waiting for me. I knew they
would be. Ian Douglas, Mouse, Henderson and Frank
Kelly. They are so excited they can't stand still. I walk
through the school gate. I am like a solitary Christian
entering the arena to face the lions. The spectators are
watching in glee.

Douglas, Henderson and Kelly have been practising. They all yell out the same words together: 'How
much pee do you put in, Headless Hopkins?'

They stagger around pretending to be peeing. Other kids are laughing too. I am cornered. And the worst thing is I still don't know how much pee you put in.

The bell monitor suddenly runs out and saves me. The bell has a long wooden handle and the monitor waves it around as if we are about to be attacked by a squadron of enemy bombers and need to run for the air-raid shelter. Everyone starts filing into the school. I have to do something to save face. As we hang our coats on the pegs in the corridor I whisper to Ian Douglas.

'I've got the skull.'

He stares at me with narrowed eyes. 'Bulldust,' he says. 'You're a liar, Headless. Always got some story.'

'I found the ladder under the pier,' I tell him. 'Like you said. It was one long pole with bits of wood nailed on.'

He falls silent. I think he believes me.

I half hope that Ian Douglas might pat me on the back. I think for a second that he might be filled with admiration at my courage. But he grabs me by the jumper with one hand and pulls my face close to his. All he says is: 'I want that skull.'

When we get inside there is a surprise. Stinker is standing out the front as usual. That is not the surprise. If it was, it would be a bad one. Not one person in the class likes him. Every boy in the room has had the

70

strap at some time or other. Even William Grey who is a brain and never makes a mistake. No, the surprise is Mr Hooper, the teacher from the Loony Bin, who is standing there on the platform with him.

What if Stinker is leaving the school and Mr Hooper is to be our new teacher? Oh, that would be fantastic.

'Hands together, Class,' barks Stinker. 'Mr Hooper has something to say to you.' We all clasp our hands on the desk in front of us. Stinker does not look as if he likes what Mr Hooper is about to say. He takes a step backwards and folds his arms. He is wearing a suit with a natty waistcoat with five buttons on the front. Mr Hooper wears a grey dust jacket. He is the only teacher I have ever seen who does not wear a suit.

Mr Hooper lets his eyes run over the class and he shines a big smile on everyone. It seems as if he is just about to talk to me and just me, but I know that everyone else is thinking the same thing.

'This class,' says Mr Hooper, 'has been picked to take part in something special.' Everyone sits up. Maybe we are going to be on the wireless or in the newspaper or something. Maybe we are going on an excursion on the train to the museum.

'You might know that I teach three days a week at Billabong,' he says.

Everyone starts to shuffle their feet or move around

uncomfortably, Billabong being the Loony Bin and all. No one wants anything to do with that place, that's for sure.

Mary Gibson, who sits behind me, once said she saw a boy from there doing something disgusting.

'What?' I asked.

Mary Gibson burst into song:

> 'Everybody's doing it, doing it.
> Pickin' their nose and chewing it, chewing it.'

I gave a shudder. If the story got around that you did such a horrible thing you would be an outcast forever. But the people in Billabong are already outcasts.

'The children in there are special,' says Mr Hooper. 'They're not as smart as you. When they are, say fourteen, they think like five year olds. They're very friendly. They're lovely people. They are like flowers in the desert. They have no meanness or cruelty in them. But at times they seem to act like babies. They go to a school inside Billabong where specialist teachers like me help them to live in the outside world.'

We all wonder what is coming next. Maybe one of us is going to be sent to Billabong? Someone dumb like me who does not even know how much pee it takes to make a baby.

'One of the boys from Billabong is going to come

to school here,' says Mr Hooper. 'In this class. It's an experiment. His parents think that he'll learn better in a regular school. And I think it will be good for you to learn next to him. These children are kind and have a lot to teach us.'

'For example?' says Stinker.

'Well,' says Mr Hooper. 'They don't tease others who are different.'

I don't agree with Mr Hooper here. The mad people in Billabong *can't* tease anyone else because they are *all* crazy. My Mum has a saying: 'It's the pot calling the kettle black.' How *could* they tease someone else for being the same as them? I shudder. I'm glad I'm not like them.

For some reason the word *Pommie* springs into my mind. I don't know why.

A murmur runs through the class. Someone says, 'loonies' under their breath and Mr Hooper hears it. Stinker tries to hide a grin.

'Loony is a terrible word,' says Mr Hooper. 'It's short for *lunatic,* which comes from the word *lunar*, which is Latin for *moon*. People once thought that the full moon made people crazy but . . .'

Mr Hooper does not get to finish the sentence because there is a loud howl coming from the corridor outside. It is like the cry of a dingo in the wild.

'Your new student's name is Victor,' says Mr Hooper.

Victor. That is the boy who wandered out the front at the Father and Son Night. He is the one who threw stones down when I was in the grave.

'We need a volunteer,' says Mr Hooper. 'We need someone to be a good friend to Victor. Someone to show him around.'

Dead silence fills the room. Everyone tries not to meet Mr Hooper's eyes. No one wants to do it. No one will play with Victor. And the poor person who gets the job of looking after him will be an outcast in the playground. I stare down at my clasped hands on the desk. In the end I have to look up. Mr Hooper is smiling. This time his smile *is* for me and me alone. I can tell he remembers me from my night of embarrassment. And he knows my name.

'Hedley Hopkins,' says Mr Hooper. 'I think *you* have what it takes to do this job.'

Sighs of relief come from every mouth. Everyone is grinning. They have escaped.

Mr Hooper walks to the door and disappears for a second or two. Then he returns holding Victor by the hand. Victor smiles as if he knows a secret joke. He is having a chuckle to himself. A bit of dribble runs out of the corner of his mouth.

'Victor, this is your new class,' says Mr Hooper. 'And Hedley is going to be your new friend.'

Looking at the class he goes on, 'This is Victor Baker.' He leads Victor down the aisle to the empty seat next to me.

'Say hello to Hedley,' says Mr Hooper.

'Say hello to Hedley,' says Victor.

Mr Hooper smiles. 'Victor just repeats what you say,' he says.

'Victor just repeats what you say,' says Victor.

There is a bit of a giggle from somewhere up the back but Stinker stops it with one of his glares.

Mr Hooper hands me an envelope. 'Hedley, this is for your parents,' he says.

I look at him with a question in my eyes. *What can be in it?*

'I want you to come to Billabong tomorrow,' he explains. 'This letter is asking permission from your parents. So you can get to know Victor in his own environment. Then he'll feel safe with you. You can become mates.'

Mates? I don't want to be friends with Victor Baker. He can't even talk properly. And he's bald. But I don't say this.

Stinker seems to be amused. He sees me looking at him and frowns. I bite my lip but I don't say anything.

My life is going down the plughole. It is bad enough now. But no one will want to be friends with me when I have Victor trailing along. Even *if* I have a skull.

Mr Hooper and Victor leave and the class gets back to normal.

I am working on a composition we started last week. Composition is writing stories and it is the only subject in school that I like. The topic is *A Windy Day*. Everyone is writing about umbrellas being turned inside out and tiles blowing off houses. I am writing a nice safe story like all the others. But at home I have written a different one which I could never let a teacher see. It is about a day when something in the drinking water makes every person in Australia break wind. The first bit goes like this:

A WINDY DAY

The North wind is hot. And foul. A great stink covers the land. The smell is worse than the Dunny Man's cart. But worst of all is the smell from a man named Stinker. Birds fall from the trees when he walks past.

I think it is a good story and one day I will let someone read it – I don't know who, though. Not Mum and Dad, that's for sure.

But at the moment I have other things to think about. Soon it will be lunchtime. I am going to be mocked about the pee. My face burns just at the thought of it.

At Warrongbool State School we have one lunchtime and two playtimes. I know I will be teased about the pee if I show my face in the playground so I spend all of this time hiding in the drum cupboard. It is dark in there but at least I am safe from Ian Douglas and the rest of them. I will be in big trouble from the teachers if I get caught because the drum cupboard is out of bounds. It is where the drums for the band are kept. The only instruments in the band are drums for the boys and fifes for the girls. No boy would ever be caught dead playing a fife and no girl would want to play the drums.

There are boys' things and there are girls' things. In Australia boys' bikes have racing handlebars which are like rams' horns and you bend down low to dodge the wind when you are going fast. Girls' handlebars are straight and the girls have to sit upright when they ride. My father bought me a new bike for my birthday but he took off the boys' handlebars and put girls' bars on instead.

'This is what they have in England,' he said. 'They are much safer.'

I begged him to put the proper handlebars back but he wouldn't.

'The boys will tease me,' I said.

'It's better than being dead from not looking where you are going,' said Dad.

I never ride the bike. It just sits in the garage slowly gathering dust.

This is not England. This is Australia. I am different from everyone else. Would I be different if I still lived back there? I am not sure. Maybe I would. I would have Granny to talk to, that's one thing. And my friend Timothy.

This is what I am thinking about when I hide in the drum cupboard again after school. I hide here until all the kids have ridden away and the playground is empty. I am scared that Ian Douglas and the others will follow me home. If Mum sees them she might find out what's in the sack. She might already have found out in which case I am as good as dead. I can't take the risk. And anyway, I want to bring it to school so that everyone will know I am the one who got it – not Ian Douglas.

Finally they have all gone. I can tell by the silence outside. I leave the drum cupboard, do up my coat against the wind and hurry home. There is no sign of Ian Douglas and his mean mates.

12

big and vicious

THAT NIGHT AT tea we all sit around the table and discuss the letter from Mr Hooper.

'Well I never,' says Mum. 'Fancy them picking Hedley.'

'I don't know about Hedley going into that place,' says Dad. 'They're all simple.'

'What do you mean?' I say.

'You know,' says Dad. 'Morons and idiots and Mongols and such. Not right in the head. Not very bright. One loaf short of a dozen.'

'That boy Victor could be dangerous,' I say.

'I like him,' says Kate. 'When he came to the

school he threw lollies at people. I saw him out of the window.'

'He can't talk properly,' I say. 'He just repeats what you say.'

'I think it's lovely,' says Mum. 'It's a great compliment to Hedley that he has been asked. They've chosen Hedley because he is a sensitive boy.'

She is right about that. I am sensitive. I don't like being called 'Pommie' or 'dumb' or 'Headless'.

'I'll come with you if you like,' says Kate.

'I'm not going,' I say.

As soon as the words are out of my mouth I know that I've made a mistake.

'You'll do as you're told,' says Dad. 'Teachers are to be respected. You have to respect authority.'

That is the end of the conversation.

The next morning I push through the shiny-leaf bush and stare in disbelief. The sack is moving. It seems to be squirming and alive. A shock of fear crashes over me as if someone has thrown a bucket of cold water in my face. I close my eyes. Is Major Manners coming back to life? That's impossible. I must be going mad. I'm heading for the Loony Bin myself for sure. What is it? I take a peep through my eyelashes.

Bull ants.

The sack is swarming with bull ants inside and out.

I must have dropped it straight on top of a nest. My heart stops racing. At least I'm not going mad. It's only bull ants. Still and all, I have a problem. They are big and vicious with long pincers growing out of their heads. If one bites you it is like being nipped with a pair of long-nosed pliers. The pain is terrible and it lasts for days. And you just can't kill them. Even if one is on the pavement and you jump on the thing with boots on, it still won't die. If you hit them with a hammer they get a bit mangled but they are still alive and trying to nip you.

I grab a twig and open the mouth of the sack. Straight away a couple of bull ants start walking along the twig towards my hand. I drop the twig with a gasp but before I do, I manage to catch a glimpse of Major Manners. The skull is seething with bull ants.

'I'm sorry, Major Manners, Sir,' I say. 'About the ants, I mean.'

I notice that the ants have eaten the little bit of skin from the top of his skull.

No worries, says a voice in my head. *Take it easy, mate. I can't feel a thing.*

Major Manners is smart and he likes me. Even though I stole him from his resting place.

'I'll get the ants off you as soon as I can,' I say. 'I have to go to the Loony Bin today.'

No such place, he says.

'You're wrong there, Sir,' I say.

Another thing, mate.

'What's that?'

Be a good sport. Don't call me Sir.

I nod my head as I turn to go. At school we have to call the teachers Sir. And Dad calls some people Sir, like his boss, Mr Brockhouse. He does not call the Dunny Man Sir. Most fathers in Australia don't call anyone Sir. Major Manners must be Australian.

I leave the sack where it is and head off towards the Loony Bin.

And my doom.

13

inside the loony bin

I ARRIVE AT the front gate of the Loony Bin at nine o'clock like it says in the letter. I am cold all over even though I am perspiring. I am wet with fear.

I have a note that tells me to report to the Office but I don't want to go inside. The tall iron gate has the words BILLABONG HOME FOR RETARDED BOYS written on it with metal letters. I am horrified to find that this gate is not locked. The loonies can get out whenever they want. Surely they must lock it at night. The beach is behind the back fence so the grave is well out of sight. But it is not out of mind.

What if the loonies kill people and bury them in the sand dunes? One of them could jump out now and cut my throat. No one would know. A quick hole in the sand and there would be no trace of me. I would be buried. Gone forever. Like Major Manners. Maybe that is what happened to him.

I am so scared.

Usually my legs decide what to do. Either I turn and run, or my feet carry me forward without instructions. But this time it is like they are nailed to the ground. I have never been this frightened before. Not even when I saw the skull for the first time.

My brain is swirling with all the terrible things that could happen to me in this place.

Stop thinking, I tell myself. Turn your thoughts to something else. I know. Count out loud. I will count my steps and push the horrible thoughts out of my head.

'One . . .

'Two . . .

'Three . . .' This is better. I am inside the Loony Bin gates getting closer to . . .

'Four . . .'

Four murderers.

'Five . . .'

Five madmen.

'Six . . .'

Six loonies.

Oh, what am I thinking about now? Counting my steps is no good. But at least I am on my way.

I stop counting and force myself to walk across the asphalt playground. There is no one around. On one side there is a double-storey building with lots of small windows. I am pleased to see that they are covered in bars. This must be where Victor Baker and the other inmates live. There is a football oval and on the other side of it a high red-brick wall. Behind that wall is probably where they keep the adult inmates. It is like a prison. I feel goose pimples running up my arm. At least I don't have to go in there.

Close to where I am standing are some long metal huts which are joined together to make up a U shape. This is the school. I can tell this by the paintings and cut-out letters that are pasted on the windows. I can hear singing coming from one of the classrooms. It is loud and mixed up with crazy laughing.

There is a sign that says HEADMASTER'S OFFICE and an arrow pointing to a door.

I step inside, trying desperately to not let my trembling legs collapse under me. I am looking at a long corridor with shiny lino on the floor. Everything is very clean but it smells of antiseptic like a hospital. I walk slowly towards the Headmaster's Office. My boots squeak on the lino and I half expect a loony to jump out and murder me for making a noise. Finally I reach the office. Inside is a big wooden desk with a typewriter on it. The Headmaster is not there.

But there *is* someone in the corridor. I go cold all over.

A weird kid is leaning against the wall. He is standing on one leg with the other tucked up under him like a seagull. I have never seen anyone with a leg as thin as this. His stomach is big and sticks out like a lady about to have a baby.

I am so scared that I can't find any words.

Finally I find my voice.

'Excuse me,' I say to Seagull Boy. 'Do you know where Mr Hooper's class is? I . . .'

'Bloody, bloody, bloody, bloody, bloody . . .'

I jump backwards and fall over. The mad boy continues to scream. He screeches so loudly that his face turns red. He yells the same word over and over.

'Bloody, bloody, bloody.'

I shuffle backwards on my bottom. This is really scary.

Seagull Boy does not move, however. In fact he doesn't even look at me. I slowly get to my feet. He doesn't attack. He is standing in the corridor outside the office. He must be in big trouble. Yes, that's what it is. In my school you would get the strap for even whispering that word. For yelling it out like that they would probably call the Police.

I stand as still as I can. If I move he might start swearing again.

My father sometimes swears when he is working in the garage. He is allowed to, but I am not. My mother doesn't know that Dad swears. If he hits his head on a cupboard he will say, 'Bloody hell.'

I once asked Mum why no one can say 'bloody' when it just means covered in blood. She said, 'It does not mean covered in blood. It stands for "By Our Lady", which is blasphemy. The Catholics don't like it at all and neither do I.'

'What's blasphemy?' I ask.

'When you say something God doesn't like,' she said. 'It's a sin. In England that word you just said is a very bad word. Over here everyone says it. But not us.'

I have just started to say 'bloody' when I talk to Ian Douglas and his gang. It makes me sound tough like them. Thank goodness Mum doesn't know I am a blasphemer.

This is what I'm thinking about while I am standing here next to the Seagull Boy who by now has fallen silent. It's funny how in dark and dangerous times my mind will wander into a different place. Mum says I have a good imagination. At other times she says I am a dreamer. Dad says I think too much.

My wanderings are interrupted by the arrival of Mr Hooper. As soon as Seagull Boy sees him he starts yelling out 'bloody' again.

Mr Hooper smiles and pats him on the shoulder. 'Good boy, Randolph,' he says. 'That is much quieter today.'

Good boy? Quieter? I just cannot figure this out.

Mr Hooper holds out his hand and I shake it. I have never shaken a teacher's hand before. It feels good. If Mr Hooper notices my fear he doesn't mention it.

'Welcome to Billabong, Hedley,' he says.

The way he says it makes me feel a bit better.

I follow Mr Hooper along the corridor to his classroom. I can't see into any of the rooms because the windows are too high. This is the same as our school. You can't look outside or into the corridor. The reason for this is to stop you staring out at interesting things when you are meant to be doing lessons, which are not interesting.

As soon as we get into Mr Hooper's classroom I can see that nothing else is like our school. For a start there are only about fifteen pupils in the room. My class has fifty-four pupils and we all sit in rows of double desks.

Each desk has two inkwells with grooves next to them where we put our pens.

The room doesn't have desks. Instead there are low tables like in infants' rooms. But the students look like they are all aged about thirteen or fourteen. Some are sitting on the floor cutting out paper shapes. Others are playing a sort of big Ludo game with numbers written on the dice. When they throw the dice they have to say the number that comes up and count it out. One group of kids is building toy aeroplanes out of scrap wood.

There are no girls in Mr Hooper's class. This must be a 'boys only' school.

In my school we all look with interest at new people who walk into the room. But these students really take a big gander when they see me. They lift their heads as a group and turn them all together. They stop talking and stare. It reminds me of a picture I once saw: a whole herd of gazelles lifting their heads at the same time as they sniffed something in the air.

'This is Hedley Hopkins,' says Mr Hooper. 'He is Victor's new friend.'

Victor comes over with a big smile.

'Hello, Victor,' I say.

'Hello, Victor,' he says happily. He puts his face right up close to mine. Too close. His nose almost touches mine.

'Victor has echolalia,' says Mr Hooper.

This time Victor does not copy the sentence. He is trying to pick something out of his teeth with a fingernail.

I have never heard this word before. It must be some terrible disease. 'What's that?' I ask.

'He repeats what you say.'

Mr Hooper holds up a toy fish. He gives it to Victor and says, 'What's this, Victor?'

'What's this, Victor?' says Victor.

Mr Hooper gives a little sigh. 'We all want him to name something. Anything,' he says. 'It would be wonderful if he could say a word or sentence which he had not copied from someone else. Just a single word of his own would mean that he was on the way to talking properly.'

Mr Hooper thinks this is important. It *is* important. The poor kid isn't a murderer. He just can't talk.

In the corner of the room is a large trunk with a padlock. Mr Hooper unlocks the trunk and takes out a hammer. He holds it up.

'Get your tools, Class,' says Mr Hooper. 'We are going to mend the hole in the fence.'

14

a gap in the fence

ALL THE BOYS rush over to a large wooden box and take out a tool each. Two of them fight over the same hammer but in the end it is sorted out. The students put on their coats and we troop outside and head off into the bushes. Mr Hooper is carrying a roll of fencing wire.

I realise with a shock where we are heading. No matter where I go or what I think, my steps and my thoughts always lead me back to the same place. And my heart is beating a little faster than it should.

One of the students named Russell is thin boned and has an enormous head. I remember him from my night in the grave. There is another boy, Michael, who is also about twelve but quite small. He sits in a folding pram with his legs twisted and his feet resting on the step.

Mr Hooper drags Michael's pram behind him as we head out into the playground. We cross the hard black asphalt space which has no trees. There is a sandpit with two sets of swings that have wooden seats held up by chains. And there's a monkey bar like the ones you see in parks which are a sort of ladder on high legs. You can swing from rung to rung like a gorilla. I've never seen a school with a monkey bar before. There's also a shelter shed just like the one in my school which smells of mouldy sandwiches. There are no flowers. There are no decorations. The buildings feel old. Not old like a palace or a mansion but old like . . . like a prisoner-of-war camp. All the buildings are faded as if the owners can't afford any bright paint.

After a bit we reach the edge of the asphalt. The whole set of buildings and yards are surrounded by small twisted ti-trees which stop people outside from staring in. I know that on the sea side where we are heading the scrub turns into sand dunes.

The wire fence with the hole in it runs through there.

And on the other side . . .

. . . is the grave.

I try to hang back but Mr Hooper urges me forward.

We push our way through this scrub. Sometimes I help lift Michael's pram when it gets bogged. Some of the other children like to bend back branches and let them whip the person behind them. This causes a lot of laughing and some crying but Mr Hooper somehow sorts everything out and keeps us moving.

Each one of these children is different and yet in some way they all seem to look alike. There is Seagull Boy with his long legs and fat stomach. And Victor with his almond-shaped eyes and stubby fingers. But then another boy, Richard, is totally different. He has long powerful arms and legs and big hands. Jeremy keeps throwing stones at things. He is a dead-eye dick. He never misses what he aims at.

Finally our journey ends. We are inside the Loony Bin property looking out through the high wire fence at the sand dunes. All the way my heart has been beating faster and faster but now it is going like the wheels of a train racing down a hill.

I stare at the grave in shock. Someone has been there. The heavy concrete slab is back in place.

Who did it?

Do they know I have the skull?

Am I being watched? Do the ti-trees hide evil eyes?

Are loonies involved?

Or murderers?

And what about Major Manners? Is his spirit lurking nearby? Will I ever hear his voice again after he finds out that I can't return his skull? The slab would be much too heavy for me to move. My racing heart has slowed and now beats like a train going *up* a hill. A great sadness sweeps over me.

A thought that I don't really want comes into my mind. Now I can give the skull to Ian Douglas with a clear conscience. I can't put it back in the grave even if I want to.

All the boys plop down on the sand as if they have just hiked a hundred miles across the desert. They pant and complain in loud voices.

'I'm knackered.'

'Puffed out.'

'Stuffed.'

There is much laughing and holding of sides. Could one of these boys be insane? A secret grave robber? No, surely not. I push the dark thoughts down into a deep space in my mind where they can't get me and concentrate on the job in hand – the hole in the fence.

Mr Hooper starts to cut pieces of wire from a roll with a pair of pliers. They remind me of the nippers on the ants crawling over Major Manners in our back garden. Gradually Mr Hooper starts to close the hole in the wire fence. One by one the others help. But they are not really helping. They bang with hammers and jab with screwdrivers but really they are just making everything worse. Richard is a real problem. He is cutting a new hole in the fence while Mr Hooper is repairing the old one.

Mr Hooper leads him to one side and gives him a long length of wire.

'Will you cut this into small pieces for me please, Richard?' he says.

Richard happily cuts the wire into pieces about one inch long. I can tell that Mr Hooper doesn't really want these pieces. It's just a smart way to keep Richard busy. All the others are banging and poking and making quite a racket. They are not doing much harm.

'Good work, everyone,' says Mr Hooper.

Good work? They are hopeless.

My father says that I am hopeless when I try to help him. Once he said that I was 'only fit for the workshop'. But these people are worse than me. *No one* would give *them* a job.

Still and all, I am starting to like them. They don't seem as if they could hurt a fly. They really are like big babies more than lunatics.

Victor, however, is being a bit of a pest.

Seagull Boy is yelling out 'Bloody, bloody, bloody.'

Victor copies Seagull Boy's last words. He is having fun. 'Bloody, bloody, bloody,' he echoes.

They stand there face to face screaming at each other. They get louder and louder. It is like a record stuck on one track. On and on and on. First one yelling and then the other. The same swear word over and over and over. All the other kids drop their tools and gather around. They laugh and laugh and laugh. They kill themselves laughing. Tears run down their cheeks. Some of them start saying 'bloody' too. I have never seen anything like it.

Mr Hooper goes over and taps Victor on the shoulder. Then he holds out his right hand to shake hands. Victor holds out his hand and Mr Hooper quickly pats him on his bald head.

'Got you,' he says.

Victor starts to cackle away like a hen. He thinks this is really funny and cocks his head to one side waiting for the next time. Victor holds his hands like someone about to catch a ball. He is not going to let this happen again.

'What's that?' says Mr Hooper.

Victor looks around but there is nothing there.

'Shake,' says Mr Hooper.

Victor holds out his hand automatically and Mr Hooper pats him on his bald head again. I can see that this is an old game between them. Victor is laughing like crazy and he has forgotten all about yelling out 'bloody'.

Nobody gets the strap. Nobody is sent to the Headmaster's Office. It is just as if nothing has happened. Weird. But smart.

Victor suddenly rushes over to Mr Hooper's toolbox and pulls out a jar. Inside is a mixture of boiled sweets. Victor shakes the jar at Mr Hooper who takes it from his hand.

'Okay,' says Mr Hooper. He hands the jar to me. 'Victor loves boiled lollies,' he says. 'But if he gets more than he can eat he throws them at people.'

Suddenly the penny drops.

My mouth starts talking before my brain can get into gear. 'That's what he was throwing when I was down the gr–'

I suddenly shut my mouth. Fool that I am. Mr Hooper stares at me with a question on his face. He throws a glance at the concrete slab, puzzled.

'Nothing,' I say. 'Sorry.'

I have just realised that when I was down in the grave Victor was throwing boiled lollies at me. Not stones. Sometimes things are not what they seem to be.

15

dog, dog, dog

'HEDLEY, TAKE VICTOR for a walk around the playground,' says Mr Hooper. 'If he wanders off, just hold out one of these lollies and he'll come back. It'll be a good chance for you to get to know each other. Don't go outside the fence though.'

Victor and I wander off from the group. He takes my hand and holds it as we walk. I'm glad that Billabong is surrounded by trees and bushes. No one can see me holding hands with another boy. I don't really mind doing it but I just don't want anyone to see me. It's sort of like a father and a little kid. I'm starting to like Victor. As we go, I name things.

'Tree,' I say.

'Tree,' says Victor.

'Sky,' I say, pointing up.

'Sky,' says Victor.

I know that this is not proper talking. He is just copying me like a little baby. Suddenly I get an idea. What if I can get Victor to say something properly? Just one word of his own. I could be the one to get him talking. Suddenly this seems really important. Worth doing. All thoughts of lunatics and idiots vanish from my mind and I start to dream about how wonderful it would be if I could get Victor to just say one word. His parents would be pleased. Wherever they are. Whoever they are. I bet they didn't really like leaving him to live in a place like Billabong Home for Retarded Boys.

A sneaky thought comes into my mind. I twist the top of the lolly jar so that it's really hard to open. Then I give it to Victor. He looks at the sweets inside – humbugs, sherbert bombs, little umbrellas covered in hundreds and thousands, lemon drops, and gob-stoppers.

'Say one word, Victor. Say the word "open" and you can have all the lollies.'

'All the lollies,' says Victor.

He tries to open the jar with his short stubby fingers. He is strong but he is clumsy. He can't get the lid off.

He struggles and strains and grows red in the face but the lid won't budge. He waves the jar in my face but I shake my head. I am not opening it unless he asks me. He starts to jump up and down making weird groaning noises. Suddenly he raises the jar high above his head.

'No,' I scream.

I am too late. Victor throws the jar down onto a rock. The jar smashes open. He falls down on his knees to get the lollies. I am really scared that bits of glass might have stuck to the lollies. I start to sweep them together with my hands but one gobstopper has rolled away a bit and Victor goes after it like a dog chasing a rabbit. In a flash it is in his mouth. But he wants more.

I shove the rest of the lollies into my pocket not worrying about any glass. 'No,' I say. 'No, Victor.'

Victor is angry and upset. Like an infant if you snatch their ice-cream. With a loud roar he turns and runs. Across the oval he goes. He is not very fast and I soon catch up and grab his coat. But he is strong. He pushes me off and I fall to the ground. He lumbers across the asphalt playground and heads for the school gate.

'Come back. Come back. I'm sorry.'

It's no good. His blood is up. In no time at all he is out the gate and running along the pavement. I am going to be in big trouble for this. What if he hurts himself?

As I run I try to wipe one of the lollies clean but it is hopeless. My fingers won't work properly while I am jogging up and down. We are running along the street past all the houses and their driveways.

Victor suddenly changes course.

'Hey, Victor,' I yell. 'Don't go in there. You'll get into trouble.'

Victor doesn't care. He is not the slightest bit worried about what people think. He doesn't live in the normal world. He charges around the back of a house. Someone lives in there. It could be anyone. A policeman. A judge. A wrestler. A criminal. But Victor doesn't give it a thought.

He has disappeared into the back garden. I stand at the gate hopelessly. This is serious. You are not allowed into other people's back gardens. If I go and try to pull Victor out he won't come. The owners might call the Police. They might say we are stealing. I can't go in but I can't leave him there either.

Without warning, a snarling noise comes from round the back. It is followed by loud barking. Oh no. They have a dog.

A big dog. An Alsatian.

Victor comes belting out of the back garden with the snarling, snapping dog at his heels. He is terrified.

'Dog, dog, dog,' he yells.

Victor hides behind me and peers around my shoulders at the Alsatian.

'Get back, you mongrel,' I yell.

This makes the dog even worse. I can see that if we turn and run it will bite one of us for sure. Slowly, slowly I start to move backwards. Victor is behind, gripping my shoulders in fright. After a bit he gets the idea and he does what I do. We take small steps backwards. It takes ages and ages of inching along but finally we reach the end of the street and the dog leaves us and goes home. All in all, we were there for about half an hour. Or more.

I walk back to Billabong with Victor holding my hand the whole way. He wipes tears from his eyes and pats my head. I can tell he likes me. I slowly start to calm down myself. I'm so glad that nothing terrible happened but I realise that we are going to be late back.

All the students are inside the classroom when we return.

'There you are,' says Mr Hooper, 'We were just about to send out a search party.'

He doesn't seem to mind us being late so I decide not to say anything about Victor running off. Stinker would have given me the strap for sure. Everyone is sitting on the mat in front of Mr Hooper who is showing them toys or pictures which he takes from a box. They are things like telephones, plastic apples, rolling pins and even a small wireless set. He hands an object or picture to someone and they have to take it and name what it is. If they get it right everybody claps. Most of them can name something. Even Seagull Boy can say something besides 'bloody'. He can name a picture of an ice-cream.

Mr Hooper gives Russell a salad bowl. Russell puts it on his head.

'Hat,' he says.

Everyone laughs and laughs. Some don't know what they are laughing about. But others do. I feel sad. The poor boy thinks a dish is a hat.

'All their food comes ready cooked,' Mr Hooper says to me in a soft voice. 'He has never seen a real kitchen. Most of these children have never been on a farm. They think milk comes out of bottles and that vegetables just appear on plates. I would like to take them to a farm one day. But it takes money. And time. And a lot of helpers.'

I feel sad about this. Why can't they live at home in a proper family?

Mr Hooper takes the bowl from Russell's head and pretends to stir with a spoon.

'Bowl,' says Mr Hooper.

'Bowl,' says Russell. Everyone claps.

Mr Hooper holds up a large pencil. 'What is this, Victor?' he says.

'What is this, Victor?' Victor replies. Mr Hooper tries not to look defeated.

Suddenly I get an idea.

'Can I have a go, please, Mr Hooper?' I say.

'Sure, Hedley,' he says.

I search through the pile of cards inside the box until I find what I am looking for. I show the picture to Victor.

'What is this, Victor?'

'Dog, dog, dog,' he yells.

Well, you wouldn't believe it. Mr Hooper starts jumping up and down and clapping.

'Well done, Victor. Well done. Good man. Great stuff.'

The whole class starts yelling and clapping and laughing. They all pat him on the back. He is a hero.

Mr Hooper is so pleased. He seems to be blinking back tears. He shakes me by the hand.

'Hedley, mate,' he says. 'You have taught Victor to talk. You have given him his voice. This is the breakthrough we've been looking for. I knew you were the right one for the job. You are amazing.'

I feel really good inside about this. For the rest of the day I help in the classroom at Billabong. At lunchtime I give out the sandwiches and apples that a nurse brings around for everyone to eat. They don't bring their own lunches like at our school. Some of them have to take pills that a nurse in a white uniform gives them.

At the end of the day I say goodbye to Mr Hooper.

'What do you think of my students now, Hedley?' he says.

'They're different,' I say. 'But they're nice.'

Mr Hooper frowns.

'So is everyone else the same then?' he asks.

I don't know what to say. For some reason I think of Bruno Ferrari, a kid in our grade who can't speak English and smells of garlic all the time. Foreigners are different. But they do know what a salad bowl is by the time they are thirteen. And they do know where milk comes from. I don't say this, though. Instead I say, 'I'm different. I'm a Pommie. And I think too much.'

My Hooper puts his hand on my shoulder and smiles.

Just then Victor comes up and gives me a big hug. He grabs me like a bear and won't let go for ages and ages. I hope that he doesn't do this tomorrow when he comes to our school.

I hold out my hand to Victor.

'Shake,' I say.

Victor holds out his hand and I pat him on the head.

We all laugh like crazy.

16

chinese burns

KATE IS IN her bedroom doing homework. She is making a picture on a piece of cloth with a thick strand of wool and a needle. At our school girls do needlework and boys do handwork like making wooden trays covered in dead matches. We have to collect the matches during the week and then glue them on in the handwork period. Kate doesn't want to talk. She doesn't like being interrupted when she is working.

Mum is cooking tea. If I go into the kitchen she'll ask me to set the table. If I'm quick I can nip down to the bottom of the garden and visit Major Manners.

I run across the lawn. The skull is in the sack where I left it. The whole thing is still crawling with bull ants. There is no way I can pick it up. I will have to get the ants off later because at any moment Mum will call me for tea.

I squat down and look at the sack from a safe distance. And I feel sad and lonely again. Tomorrow I am going to give the skull to Ian Douglas and then Major Manners will never be laid to rest. Goodness knows what the gang will do with him. Something horrible, that's for sure.

'Sorry, Major Manners,' I say. 'I know you should be back in your grave. But if I hand you over I'll have some friends.'

A picture of Timothy comes into my mind. He used to live next door to me in England. We used to swap *Beano* comics. In the winter we would splash around in puddles in our Wellingtons together. He knew what Wellingtons were. Over here no one has ever heard of Wellingtons. They call them gumboots. When I told Dad this he shook his head and gave me a lecture all about Lord Wellington who was the first one to wear long boots. Wellington defeated Napoleon who was a Frog. Dad calls the French 'Frogs' because he doesn't like them.

'We saved them in two World Wars and they still aren't grateful,' he said.

When I asked him what this had to do with gum-boots, he snorted, 'Do you think it was Lord Gumboot who beat Napoleon at Waterloo?'

I am wandering again. All this started off because I told Major Manners I need some friends.

You already have friends, he says. *You have Victor.*

'Victor is simple,' I say. 'He doesn't know much. He is not like everyone else.'

Are you like everyone else? Is anyone? says the voice in my head.

I think about this. I am not like everyone else. I talk differently to the other children. And I am not really good at anything at school. Except Composition. I am no good at Times Tables. When we have Tables, Stinker stands at the front of the class and spits them out like a snake striking a mouse. He doesn't even say your name. He just points to you and you have to give the answer.

'Seven tens?'

'Four threes?'

'Nine elevens?'

'Eight nines?'

I hate the nines. I can never get the nines correct. Especially eight times nine. For some reason Stinker always asks me the nines. If you get one wrong he raps you over the fingers with a ruler and it hurts.

Seventy-two, mate, says Major Manners. *Turn it around the other way. Nine eights. Ten eights is eighty so take away one eight and bingo – seventy-two.*

Major Manners is smart and he likes me, so I don't tell him that when Stinker is spitting out the Tables you are filled with terror and don't have time to think about little tricks in your mind. I have heard the one about turning the Tables around before.

Just then Mum calls out my name.

'Tea time, Hedley,' she yells out through the kitchen window.

'See you later, Major Manners,' I say.

See you later, mate, he says. *And . . .*

'Yes?'

You're a nice kid. Just remember that. Be nice to yourself.

'Thanks,' I say.

I hurry inside and take my place at the table. Someone else has set it. Mum or Kate but definitely not Dad who often goes and sits on the toilet when there are jobs in the kitchen. He does this when the washing-up is to be done. He takes a book into the toilet and somehow or other always seems to come out just when the washing-up is finished.

'Watch this,' Mum said one night. She filled the kitchen sink up with water and waited for a couple of minutes. Then she pulled out the plug. There was a loud gurgling noise as the water ran out of the sink. Dad immediately came out of the toilet. His face fell when he saw the dirty dishes still on the table.

'Got you,' said Mum.

We all laughed but Dad didn't think it was funny. He stomped off to the garage.

Tonight for tea it is oxtail soup made in the pressure cooker. It is served up with dumplings which are sort of doughy cakes that are not sweet. I love oxtail soup but I'm not crazy about the dumplings. I eat them, however, because at our place it is: 'eat everything or get nothing'. This includes ice-cream.

'How did your day at Billabong go, dear?' says Mum. 'I'm ever so proud of you being picked to be the one to look after Victor.'

I open my mouth to answer but Dad gets in first and tells a story about a simple man who works in his factory. His story goes on and on and on, but he finally finishes up with . . .

'The poor bloke left a tap running when he went home. In the morning the whole place was flooded. I had to give him the sack. *He* was simple. A dill. Not good for anything.'

I quickly try to say something. 'This boy Victor –'

'Speaking of boys,' says Mum. 'There are four

of them loitering outside.' She is staring out of the window. 'They don't look very nice.'

I peep out through the net curtains and see Ian Douglas and his mates lurking by the letterbox. My heart sinks.

'Are they your friends?' says Mum.

'No,' I say. 'But I know who they are.'

'Tell them to go away,' she says. 'They look common.'

I walk out to the letterbox which in Australia is attached to the garden fence and not set into the front door like in England. My mind has a billion thoughts which swirl around like all the ingredients in the sloppy cake-mix my mum stirs with a wooden spoon at Christmas.

I can't let them have Major Manners. He is my friend. But he is only a bone. And everyone will admire me when they know I have stolen him. I could swear at the gang and act tough. But they are tougher. I could run away. But I will have to come home again in the end.

I could scare them. But how? An idea comes into my head as I reach the gate.

'Where's the skull, Headless?' says Ian Douglas.

'Hidden,' I say.

'Get it.'

'I can't. I'm not allowed out. My mum wants you to go away.'

Henderson turns to Frank Kelly. '*My mum wants you to go away*,' he repeats in a put-on voice. 'Oh, diddums.'

The others laugh cruelly.

'It's dangerous,' I say.

'What is?'

'The skull.'

'It's evil,' I say. 'It talks to me. Its eyes get red in the dark. It comes from Hell. It makes me do what it says.'

For just a moment there is a small doubt in their eyes. I warm up to my story.

'It wants me to lead you to the grave. It's the entrance to Hell. The Devil is waiting for the skull's victims.'

Ian Douglas nods his head as if he is a very wise person giving this some thought.

'Like in *Inner Sanctum*,' he says. 'Yeah, I read that comic too, Headless. Good try.'

The others look at me as if I'm pathetic.

'Next it will be howling at the moon in the dead of night,' says Henderson.

'A full moon, of course,' says Frank Kelly.

They all laugh in a mean way.

I give up my silly attempt at trying to scare them. 'Look,' I say. 'I think we should put it back. What if the Police find out?'

'Who's going to tell them?' says Ian Douglas.

'My parents.'

For a second he looks worried. 'You haven't told them, have you, you idiot?'

I think of saying 'yes' but I know this won't save me. So far the gang haven't done anything wrong. I am the one who took the skull. If adults get involved the gang will tell on me. I would be the only one to get into trouble.

'No,' I say. 'But my mother is watching. She wants you to go away.'

They look over to the window of our house and sure enough, there is Mum staring out through the net curtains with a disapproving look.

'Bring it to school tomorrow. Or else.' Ian Douglas says this last bit through his teeth. It sounds really scary.

The gang mooch off into the evening, mumbling something about giving me a Chinese burn.

A Chinese burn is when someone grabs you by the wrist with two hands and twists your skin in different directions. It hurts like crazy. But not as much as being bitten by bull ants. I hope Major Manners is all right down there at the bottom of the garden. He should be safe. I tell myself that the bull ants will stop anyone touching him.

17

a fiendish plan

THAT NIGHT I toss and turn in bed. I have to figure out a way of getting rid of the bull ants so that I can take Major Manners to school. I have to get them off before morning. But I can't do anything until Mum and Dad are asleep. I lie there thinking about all my troubles, trying not to fall asleep. My eyes are heavy and I know there is a danger that I will nod off if I'm not careful.

I make plans. I will sneak down to the kitchen and grab a torch and a jar of honey. Then I will tiptoe down to Major Manners and make a trail of honey leading away from the sack. I can pour a pool of honey in the grass and the bull ants will follow the trail to it and leave Major Manners alone. When morning comes he'll be free of ants and I can grab the sack and take it to school.

Brilliant. I am a genius if I do say so myself. It is a fiendish plan. I lie in the dark smiling to myself. A great feeling of relief floods through me. Soon this whole problem will be over. I am still a bit sad about Major Manners but I can't get him back into the grave anyway. So everything will be all right. He will understand.

After ages and ages the house falls silent. Mum and Dad are safely asleep. I creep along to the kitchen and open the fridge. I can't turn the light on because I don't want to disturb Mum and Dad but a dim glow comes out of the fridge and softly lights the room. I grab the jar of honey, which is all sticky from Kate pinching spoonfuls when no one is around. I take Dad's torch out of the bottom drawer in the kitchen bench and head out into the dark night.

It is cold and dark and the grass is damp. Bits of new-mown grass are sticking to my slippers. I should have put on my dressing-gown but it's too late to go back now. I shiver inside my pyjamas and hurry on. This won't take long.

Suddenly I feel something under my foot.

Something long and thin.

A snake.

'Aaagh,' I give a terrible scream, jump backwards and fall heavily onto my backside.

The honey jar goes flying into the air. It comes down and hits me on the chest and then rolls down over my legs onto the grass.

I push myself backwards like a baby shuffling on its bottom. I hate snakes. They are deadly poisonous.

It is a really long snake. The longest one in the world.

In fact it is not a snake at all . . .

It is only the garden hosepipe.

I sit there shaking and nervously looking back at the house. All is silent. All is well.

No it's not. My pyjamas and slippers are covered in honey. And the jar is half empty. I am going to get into big trouble for this. Why does everything have to go wrong all the time?

All is not lost, though. I can still make the honey trail to attract the ants away from Major Manners.

But where is the torch? I search around on my hands and knees. I can't find it. It is too dark. I would give anything for a full moon even if it brought out a few full-moon murderers. Nothing is important except getting the skull to school. I continue to search around but the torch is nowhere to be found. And I keep thinking about snakes. Soon my sticky pyjamas are covered in grass and twigs. I am never going to be able to explain this when Mum finds my pyjamas in the wash.

I feel my way down to the shiny-leaf bush without the torch to guide me. There in the gloom is the dull shape of the sack. I can just make it out. I can sense, rather than see, the swarming mass of bull ants. I bend over and start to pour a little trail away from the skull. It's difficult work because I can't see anything. Am I pouring too much or am I pouring too little? I just don't know. I'm squatting down, shuffling along with my backside close to the ground. It's taking an awfully long time. I'm not even sure that there is any honey left in the jar.

A feeling comes over me. I know that something is wrong. My brain is telling me that it is.

Careful, cobber, says Major Manners from inside the sack. *Ants love honey*.

I freeze. I am not just wearing pyjamas any more. I can sense it. I am wearing a coat of swarming bull ants.

I burst out of the bushes like a tiger leaping out of the jungle. *Ouch*. A needle of pain shoots through my left hand. I brush off the bull ant and start dancing around. They are all over my sticky pyjamas going for the honey. Frantically I start undoing the buttons on my top. *Ouch, ouch, ouch*. More bites. I am dancing around desperately trying to undo the buttons. One, two, three. I can't take this any more. I rip the top of my pyjamas off sending buttons popping into the night.

Ouch, ouch, ouch.

In a flash I have my pyjama pants off too. I run, silently screaming, towards the house. There is one thing I need more than anything.

Light.

I race naked across the lawn, hoping nobody sees me, and in the kitchen door. Then I run down the hall to my bedroom and flick the light switch. I examine my bare body. One ant. One ant only. The rest are out there on the grass all over my pyjamas and Major Manners' skull.

I carefully pull my index finger back with my thumb and aim it at the bull ant. Flick. It spins across the room and lands on my bedside table. Quick as a flash I grab the empty glass nearby and place it over the ant. It's trapped.

'Are you all right, Hedley?' comes Mum's voice.

I quickly switch off the light and jump into bed, starkers.

'Just getting a drink,' I yell.

The house falls silent. A feeling of failure and doom

falls over me as I pull the sheets up. I start to scratch the bull-ant stings. I just want to go and tell my mother everything. I want her to take over and say that she will look after me and everything will be all right. I want her to make all my troubles go away. But this is not the way it would be if I told her. There would be police stations and angry teachers and talk about vandals and punishment.

Time passes slowly but eventually I start to settle down a bit. Maybe in the morning the ants will have left the skull and be on my pyjamas. Maybe none will be on Major Manners. Maybe my plan will still work.

Maybe.

18

terrible magic stirring

I LIE THERE naked in bed scratching my bull-ant bites. They have stopped throbbing but are itchy. I have a bad one right between my legs, high up on one thigh just under my balls. I scratch the bite gently. The next thing I know I have a stiffy. And right at this moment, for some unknown reason the vision of a naked lady comes into my mind.

Before long I am having a daydream – no – a night dream about naked breasts. I let my mind wander. I love thinking about naked ladies but I know it's wicked. No Soldier of Jesus would ever let such sinful thoughts into their mind. The Gates of Hell must be wide open waiting for me.

I have to stop thinking like this. It is wrong. What if Mum could read my thoughts? What if she knew I was thinking about breasts? She has probably never even heard the word 'tits' which is what Ian Douglas calls them.

Don't think about breasts, Hedley. Think about fishing or books. Yes, books. What is a good book? I know – *Biggles Flies North*. Then another title pops into my mind – *Madness at Midnight*. The one with the naked lady on the cover I saw in the shop. There I go again. I can see that lady now with the man's top hat in the way of the interesting bits. Oh, my stiffy is really stiff. It feels good. It really does. I close my eyes. I see naked women. Twelve of them.

'Don't think it. Don't think it,' I desperately tell myself. But it does no good. I can't stop. Thoughts and sights just come pouring into my mind.

The twelve naked ladies come dancing into the room. They are in a Conga line and they throw their arms into the air. There are redheads and brunettes and blondes. They are so happy and they are putting on their naked dance just for me. Their breasts bounce up and down as they dance. It's almost as if God has sent them to give me my dearest wish. And yet Rev Carpenter says it's the Devil who brings such thoughts. On and on they dance around my bed.

Oh, I would love to hug one of these ladies.

I grab my pillow and wrap my arms around it with my eyes tightly shut.

Somewhere deep inside my guts I feel a terrible magic stirring. It's like I am being thrown up at the sun. I feel a wicked shudder of pleasure erupting from within me.

Ah, blimey. I am wetting myself.

I have wet the bed.

No I haven't.

I switch on the light and see that this sticky white stuff is all over the pillow and my stomach. What in the hell is it? What have I done? God has got me. I am diseased. I have shot out pus from my rotting insides.

Have I caught Leprosy or the Black Death from the skull? Is this God's way of showing me his anger? Am I dying? I've ruined my whole life before it's even started. Oh God, forgive me. I will never think of naked ladies again. I promise. Just make me better. Oh, please make me better.

I hear a noise from the kitchen. Oh no. Mum is up. What's she doing up? If she comes in and finds me like this she will erupt like a pressure cooker blowing its valve. Her fury will be like scalding steam.

I grab a handkerchief and start wiping down the white goo on the pillow and my stomach. It smells funny. Like the water in the public swimming pool.

Mum will know that this stuff has come out of my stiffy from evil thoughts. Or a disease I've caught from a diseased skull. I quickly grab an empty tin and shove the soggy handkerchief inside. It's a nougat tin. I close the lid and hide the tin under the socks in my clothes drawer.

I quickly pull on a clean pair of pyjamas and look around. The naked ladies have gone. They are a million miles away. I will never let them back inside my head. Never, never, never.

God, please forgive me.

Finally I fall asleep. I have a terrible dream. It's a dream that I've had many times before. In the dream I am standing at the top of the staircase in our tiny house in England. At the bottom of the stairs is an ocean with huge passenger liners leaving the shore. I start to tumble down the stairs over and over and over until I splash heavily into the water. On the shore an old lady is waving to me sadly. She wants to help but she can't. I wake up at this point in the dream. I'm shaking with fear.

The dream reminds me of the boat we came to Australia on. My granny was going to come with us but the night before the ship left she had a dream that she was going to die on the boat. So she wouldn't come. Granny was left behind and went to live in an old people's home.

I miss Granny. We used to go on walks together across the park. I could tell her things. No matter how bad it was or how foolish, she never scolded me.

The boat we came on was lots of fun. It was full of other English people moving to Australia to live. They all wanted to come here. Not like the early convicts who were brought out in chains. Our trip took five weeks so they had a school on the boat to keep the children out of mischief.

When we reached the Suez Canal in Egypt, they had a fancy-dress competition for all the kids. Some were dressed as King Neptune or sea monsters. There were a lot of Arabs and ghosts because all you needed was a white sheet. We had to parade around in a circle and the teacher on the boat gave us points to see who would win.

Kate and I were not very interesting at all. We just had words pinned all over us so that we looked like walking noticeboards.

Mine said: ENGLAND – RAIN and SLEET, RATIONING, NO MEAT, NO PETROL, NO SMOKES, BLOOD SWEAT and TEARS.

Kate's said: AUSTRALIA – SUNSHINE and SURF, FULL

When Kate walked out behind me everyone cheered. No one cheered for me and I wasn't sure why.

Dad said, 'Don't take it personally. You are the past. She is the future.'

The Suez Canal was like a long straight river running through the desert. All the little white English children went out to play in the swimming pool at the front of the boat. Dad wouldn't let us out of the cabin because Arabs had come on board the ship to check things out while we went through the Canal. Dad said the Arabs might kidnap us. He was the only person who thought this and we were the only kids who could not go out and swim.

The following day the other children were screaming and crying with pain. Their pale white skin was as red as the Arabs' hats and they had huge blisters the size of golf balls all over their bodies. They had terrible sunburn. When one of their blisters burst a clear liquid ran out all over their skin.

You are not supposed to get fluid coming out of your skin. And you are not supposed to get white stuff coming out of your stiffy when you think about naked ladies.

19

out of the sack

IN THE MORNING my mind is full of fear. I can't stop thinking about the terrible things that are going on in my life. I have a disease. Ian Douglas is waiting for the skull. The only thing I can do is to take Major Manners to school and be a hero. I don't really want to do it but I have no choice.

I look at the bull ant under the glass next to my bed. My first thought is to kill it. But I will have to cut it up or squash it with a hammer. Somehow I just can't bring myself to do this so I slip a piece of paper under the glass and carry the ant outside. I let it go on the grass near the rotary clothes line.

'Good luck,' I say.

My pyjamas have gone. Maybe a dog or a cat has carried them off. There is going to be trouble when Mum finds out. I wonder if the ants stung the dog or cat. The jar of honey is still on the grass and it is covered in ants. It is nearly empty and has bits of grass stuck all over it. The torch is lying nearby. I pick up the torch and kick the jar under a bush. Then I make my way down to see Major Manners. What will I find?

A feeling of dread seeps over me. Will the sack be gone? I walk slowly, just in case the answer to this question is 'yes'. I am sort of putting off the dreadful moment. At last I reach the shiny-leaf bush.

'Yes.'

I mean 'no'. The sack is still there. The skull has not been carried off. But it is still crawling with bull ants. I know from what has happened that there is no way I will be able to get rid of them before I go to school. Think, think, think. What can I do?

Just then I hear Mum's voice. 'Hedley, what are you doing down there? You will be late for school again – it's five-and-twenty past eight. I have to go to a Mothers' Union meeting. Lock up the house before you leave. Kate's waiting. Come on, shake a leg.'

My mind goes into top gear. I have to get the ants off the skull or I can't take it to school. How can I do it? I can't remove them with a brush or a rag because they are too fierce and they will bite me. I could put Major Manners into a bucket of water. That might get them off, but I doubt it. A lot of the ants are inside the skull and it will take ages for them to drown. There isn't enough time. Kate is already waiting for me at the front gate talking to her friends but she won't go without me.

I will just have to leave the skull and come back for it at lunchtime.

I run inside to get my lunch from the fridge. Mum always makes our sandwiches the night before so that there is not too much of a rush in the morning. While I am looking in the fridge I suddenly get an idea. I look in the freezing compartment. There is a brick of ice-cream in there. Neopolitan – the sort with stripes of different colour. I put the cardboard container on the kitchen table. Next I grab a coathanger from the hall cupboard and straighten it out. I make a little hook on the end.

I rush down to the shiny-leaf bush. I lift up the ant-covered sack with my piece of bent wire. The bull ants go crazy but I manage to shake out the skull. It rolls across the ground like a bowling ball.

'Sorry, Major Manners,' I say.

Careful, mate, he replies. He calls me 'mate' a lot.

'I have to take you to school. But first I will get the ants off.'

Aren't you going to take me back to rest in peace in my grave? he says.

'I can't,' I say.

The bull ants are swarming up the wire towards my hands. I hook the wire through Major Manners' eye socket and run for the house. Anyone would think I was carrying a live bomb that was about to explode.

'Ouch, oh blimey.'

A bull ant has bitten me on the finger. I drop the skull and flick the ant off my skin. Then I jump up and down shaking my hand. Oh crikey, it hurts. It feels as if someone has shoved a red-hot needle into my flesh.

'That hurt,' I yell.

You're telling me nothing, says Major Manners.

I leave the wire on the ground and look around. A broom is leaning against the wall near the back tap. Just the shot. I grab the broom and shove the handle into the hole at the bottom of the skull. Then I race into the kitchen.

The fridge is still open and so is the freezing compartment. I shove the ant-covered skull into the space where the ice-cream was and shut the freezer compartment. I close the fridge and leave the broom by the door.

Brilliant. I am very proud of myself. The ants will all freeze to death while I'm at school. I can race back at lunchtime and get the skull then.

'Hurry up, Hedley, we –' comes Kate's voice. She is coming through the front door.

'All right, all right,' I yell. 'Keep your shirt on.'

I race outside and head for school with Kate. Her friends have gone.

All the way there I am worried.

I don't have the skull. And Ian Douglas will be waiting for me. I can only think about one thing. Chinese burns.

20

running away

KATE GOES INTO school but I do not. There is a trick which every kid who is being bullied uses to stop enemies getting them before school. You hide outside until the bell has gone. Then, when the last kid has just gone inside, you quickly run up and walk in behind them. This saves you from getting caught. Until play-time that is. But if you get it wrong and make yourself late you will get the strap from your teacher.

As I hurry in and hang my hat and coat on the peg I see Mr Hooper. He is leaving after having brought Victor to school. He puts one hand on my shoulder and says, 'Victor is saying more and more words all the time. He is so proud of himself. The other kids have been teaching him as well. They all want to teach him new words. It's amazing what he can name already. Gees, Hedley, mate. You have done so well.'

I go into the classroom and sit down. Victor is in his seat sitting next to me in my two-seater desk. My new friend.

Ian Douglas raises an eyebrow. He wants the skull. Stinker is looking at me as if he is just going to ask me what nine eights are. Victor grins at me crazily. He is dribbling from his mouth. I am ashamed of my thoughts but I can't help it. Victor is embarrassing.

'Well, Hopkins,' says Stinker. 'I believe you have been giving Victor language lessons. What words does he know? Show us your new-found skill.'

'Victor,' I say. 'Tell us a word.'

I see his lip tremble and for a second I think he is going to say 'Tell us a word'. But he doesn't. Victor jumps up and bends over. His backside is pointing at my face.

'Fart,' he yells. He lets rip with the biggest, longest fart I have ever heard.

The whole class breaks up. There is nothing that breaks a class up like a fart. This is true in England as well. Even a mean teacher like Stinker can't stop the hoots of laughter that flood the classroom.

Victor is the loudest laugher of all. He thinks he has done something brilliant. He laughs with a huge wide open mouth. So does everyone else. Victor is laughing with the class. But they are laughing *at* him. And at me.

The whole nightmare reminds me of Luna Park fairground where laughter is played out of all the loudspeakers in the Giggle Palace and the open clown mouth at the entrance. The world can hear it bouncing off the sky.

Somebody else in the classroom farts and the laughter doubles. Now Stinker does not think it is amusing. The class is getting out of control. Whoever did that fart is in for big trouble.

'Heads on desks,' shouts Stinker.

This order means we have to cross our arms on the desk and place our faces down on them so that we can't see anything. Everyone does what they are told but shoulders are shaking with the effort of trying to stop the laughter. Suddenly someone lets go with another loud snort and all the others lose control. It is like trying to stop a river with your fingers. Because our heads are down, the laughing echoes under the desk and fills the whole room with an incredible roaring sound.

'Stop this. Stop this,' yells Stinker. 'I am getting my strap out of the cupboard.'

The laughter turns to giggles but still does not stop.

'Bum,' says Victor. It gets a roar from the class. I turn my head and peep at Victor. He doesn't have his head down on his hands like the rest of us. He is very impressed by the laughter the last word aroused, and is staring around wildly.

Shrieks of mirth erupt from the bent heads. Victor is beside himself with happiness.

'Poop,' says Victor.

The laughing doubles again.

'Tits,' says Victor. Everyone gives up keeping their head down. It is too much effort. Henderson laughs so much that he actually falls out of his desk.

Victor is saying all the naughty words the other kids at Billabong have told him. Goodness knows what he will say next. Another voice speaks out.

'Hopkins.'

Through the din I hear my name. But it's not Victor who says it. It is Stinker.

He roars down the aisle and grabs me by the scruff of the neck with one hand. In his other hand he holds his thick leather strap. Now everyone falls silent. This is serious. No one knows who could be next. He throws me stumbling onto the platform at the front of the class.

'Hopkins,' he yells. 'You think flatulence is funny? I'll teach you to break wind in my class. I am going to

135

teach you a lesson you won't forget in a hurry.'

'It's not my fault, Sir,' I say. 'I didn't do it.'

His face is red and his mouth is foaming like a horse. 'Don't talk back to me, boy,' he yells. 'Hold out your hand.'

He is going to give me six of the best.

I have had enough of this. I don't care if he is a teacher. I don't care if he is appointed by God himself. This is wrong.

'Don't touch me,' I yell. I can't believe I am saying this, but it's not fair. 'It's not my fault that the class can't stop laughing.'

'Hold out your hand,' shrieks Stinker. Everyone has fallen silent now. They put themselves in my place in their minds. It is not a place they would like to be.

'No,' I shout. 'You are not giving me the strap. You are a horrible, mean . . .'

'Shit.'

The missing word has been provided by Victor. He is grinning, still looking for laughs. But his word hangs in the silence. It almost seems as if *I* have provided the missing word.

Stinker lashes out at my legs with his strap. But I jump. He grabs me by the collar and whips at my legs. My socks are hanging down around my ankles. If only I had put on my garters they would have held my socks up and given me some protection. The strap curls around my leg as it hits. The pain is terrible. Hot and hard.

One . . .

Two . . .

Three . . .

'Stop, stop,' I cry.

Four . . .

Five . . .

Six . . .

Seven . . .

My mind starts to swirl. I remember the talk in the playground. Teachers are only allowed to give you six by law. And not on the legs.

Eight . . .

Nine . . .

Ten . . .

Oh, it hurts. I am not taking any more. I kick Stinker in the shin. He lets go with a shriek and stares at me in disbelief. He is panting like an enraged bull ready to charge. But he won't get me. I turn. And run for it.

I leave that classroom like a cork out of a pop-gun. I belt across the asphalt playground and out of the steel gates. I race down the quiet streets past the watching houses. I leave that school like a boy running from teachers and a loony and the Police and the strap of a cruel man. I leave like a lunatic. I leave like that because that's who I am. I am a loony on the run. My life is a total disaster.

I have no friends, I've caught a terrible disease, I made a fool of myself about the pee, I've stolen a skull and I have run off from school. The back of my legs are burning. They are already turning purple and blue.

Soon they will put out a search party. I have to get back to Major Manners before they do. Does the Head-master call the Police if a boy runs away from school? I don't know. I kicked a teacher in the shin. The teachers will come after me for sure. Ian Douglas will tell them that I have the skull. I am a criminal now.

The streets are quiet because all the children are in school. If you are out of school with your parents when everyone else is hard at work in the classroom you feel terrific in this quiet, unusual world. But if you are on the run you feel like a criminal. You are not meant to be here. You are unusual. You are weird.

My school boots pound the footpath loudly as I run. *Skull, skull, skull*, they seem to say. Why does Ian Douglas want Major Manners? Is it just to make himself look big in front of everyone? Or does he want to use him for some sort of ritual with his gang? Like in *Inner Sanctum* where a cult of naked people dance around a skull before throwing it into a bonfire.

Suddenly I make a big decision. They can do whatever they like to me. I am alone in the world except for Major Manners. No one cares except him. He is my friend. Dead, yes. But sometimes he speaks inside my brain. I have to look after him. More than that – I have to take him back to the grave.

I run even faster.

'Major Manners,' I say. 'I won't be long.'

21

a wild man

AS I THUNDER into our front garden I hear loud footsteps behind me. I dodge around the back of the garage and press myself against the wall. Was someone following me? Ian Douglas? Stinker? The Police? Or was it just someone running along the road because they were late for a bus?

I creep up to the kitchen door.

All my senses are alert. I am like a mouse who knows there is a cat somewhere in the room. Suddenly there is a loud crash from inside. It sounded like someone dropping something heavy on the floor. Burglars. Burglars must have come to rob the house.

Another thought comes into my mind. Ian Douglas and the others. They have come for the skull. They must be inside the house at this very moment.

I rush into the kitchen. What I see does not make sense. It is sort of like looking at one of those squashed ink-blot pictures where you have to try and make something out of it. I see what I see but my mind just can't take it in. It's probably only a few seconds but it seems like hours. Finally I manage to understand.

My mother is lying on the floor. Well, not lying. She is sort of crumpled as if someone has taken the bones out of her legs and she has just collapsed. Her eyes are closed and she looks as if she is dead.

Next to her on the floor is a cardboard box with pink and white and green ice-cream flowing out of it.

The fridge door is open and so is the freezing compartment.

Staring out at us is a frozen skull, covered in frozen bull ants.

My brain, which is also frozen, starts to thaw. Mum must have seen the melted ice-cream and gone to put it back in the fridge. When she opened the freezing compartment she saw a skull covered in frozen bull ants staring out at her.

Then she had a heart attack and died.

Oh, what have I done.

'Mum, Mum, Mum,' I cry.

There's no response. I lift up her head but it's floppy. What can I do? Should I turn her over and try to get her breathing by pressing on her back like the life-savers do when someone has drowned? Does she have a pulse? I try to remember first aid from school. I just can't get my brain to think properly.

Her eyelids start to flutter. She is not dead. She has fainted. Phew.

And she is waking up. Quick, quick, quick. I must get rid of the skull before she sees it again. I grab the broom, which is still where I left it over by the door, and shove it into the base of the skull. I hold it up straight so that it doesn't fall off.

Mum opens her eyes and looks at me.

What does she see? She sees her son standing there like a wild cannibal from years gone by. I must look like an ancient head-hunter with his prize fixed on the end of a pole. Mum sits up on the floor.

'Hedley Hopkins,' she screams at me. 'You wicked boy. What have you done?'

My mouth is hanging open like one of those plastic clowns which are lined up next to each other at Luna Park. People drop table-tennis balls into their mouths to see if they can win a prize. I move my head from side to side like the clowns but nothing comes into my mouth or out of it. I am speechless. And I am wicked.

My mother often uses this word. She has a little saying about me which she often repeats:

> When he is good he is very, very good.
> But when he is bad he is wicked.

I am wicked. I am a wicked person. Bad. Sinful.

And I am not alone in the kitchen with my mother. There is another person there. He bends down and peers into my mother's face. Then he puts one finger against her nose and presses it.

'Nose,' he says.

It is Victor. He grins at me. Then he grins at the skull on top of the broom handle. Victor has followed me home. His were the footsteps I heard behind me. Mr Hooper told him to stay close to me and that is what he's done. My mother stares up at him in fear and amazement.

How can I explain all this? Soon Mr Hooper and Stinker and the Police will arrive. No one will believe that I didn't break open the lead coffin and take out the skull. I know it was Ian Douglas and the gang who did it. But they will never own up. Everyone will call me a vandal. They will say that nothing is sacred. They might even read my mind and know that I've been thinking about naked ladies.

If I stay here I'll be caught. I could be put in prison. My picture might be in the paper because I am a criminal.

Will I run for it? Or will I stay and face up to what I have done?

Suddenly my mind is made up for me. Victor grabs the broom from my hands and holds the skull up high. He rattles it above his head. Then he gives an enormous wild cry and runs out of the door. He is taking Major Manners. He is rushing off with my friend.

'Head,' he yells. 'Head.'

When Victor first saw the skull back at the grave he was terrified. But not now. My friendship with him seems to have changed all that. Now it is *my* turn to be scared. Scared of losing Major Manners.

'Come back,' I scream. 'Come back, you idiot.'

I race out of the door after him.

Behind me I hear Mum calling out, but I can't make out the words. A louder voice is speaking inside my head. It must be Major Manners.

The voice says, *You are using this as an excuse to run. You should stay and tell the truth. There's nothing to be ashamed of. You're running away again.*

The voice is only small and in a second I have shoved it down inside my own skull. I am belting down the street after Victor. He comes to a halt at the bus stop where an old lady is standing next to her shopping cart. The cart is like a pram without a baby – all the mothers have them. Mum has one just the same which she takes to the shops and loads up with the week's food.

The old lady starts to tremble as she is faced by Victor – a wild bald crazy kid who is laughing like a baby being tickled. He leaps around with the skull on the end of the broom handle. Victor suddenly grabs a loaf of bread out of her basket and yells out, 'Bread'.

Before she can even scream he puts back the bread and is off again, down the road towards the beach.

'Hedley,' comes an urgent voice from behind me. 'Hedley, wait for me.'

I do not wait. I follow Victor and Major Manners.

And Kate follows me. What is *she* doing here?

Victor charges down the road with the skull on the end of the broom handle. Everyone stares at the weird sight. Whenever Victor sees something that he recognises, he names it at the top of his voice.

He grabs the handlebars of a postman's bike and yells out, 'Bike.'

He races into a public toilet holding his skull up high. Oh, what? It is the Ladies' side.

'Dunny,' he yells. He is out again in a flash, thank goodness.

He names everything in our crazy world.

'Bus.'

'Tree.'

'Butcher.'

'Pier.'

'Sand.'

'Bird.'

'Dog, dog, dog.'

22

wagging it

KATE AND VICTOR and I are on the beach and we are playing truant from school. 'Wagging it', as they say in Australia. And we are not the only ones doing it. There is a tiny terrier wagging its tail and chasing seagulls. It pauses to look at us. Victor is scared. The dog senses his fear and starts to yap. Victor stops running and hides behind me. He is trembling, making the skull on the end of the broom rattle like a set of false teeth tied to a branch in a storm.

'It won't hurt you, Victor,' I say.

'Shoo,' yells Kate. She charges at the dog and it turns tail and runs.

I gently take Victor's hand and lead him to a sand dune where the three of us sit down. Victor glances nervously at the dog which is now chasing seagulls along the pier.

Kate stares at the skull.

'What's going on, Hedley?' says Kate. 'Did he steal that from the grave?' She gives a little shudder.

For just a second I think about letting Victor take the blame. It would get me off the hook.

Tell the truth, says Major Manners.

'No,' I say. 'I did.'

Kate's mouth falls open. 'Hedley,' she gasps. 'You promised me. You said you wouldn't go back there.'

'It's a dare,' I say.

I know this explanation sounds weak and the look on Kate's face tells me that she thinks so too. I can just hear myself saying 'it's a dare' to the judge when the Police take me to court.

'I told Ian Douglas and his gang that whatever they said I would do it.'

'That's crazy,' says Kate. 'What for?'

Victor rattles the skull on the end of the broom handle.

'To make friends.'

'No one needs friends like them,' says Kate.

'Everyone needs at least one person,' I say.

'What about Victor?' she says. 'Isn't he your friend?'

'Victor doesn't count,' I say.

'Why not?'

'He is just a little kid in a big body. He wouldn't hurt anyone. None of them would. But he doesn't know much. He's . . . simple.' Victor is listening. He doesn't understand but he nods his head as if he does.

'Friend,' says Victor.

Kate stares at the little dog that is running along the pier. 'What's man's best friend?' she says.

I'm not quite sure what she's asking me this for. 'A dog?' I answer, remembering the old saying. Kate nods.

'Victor knows a lot more than a dog,' she says.

I don't answer for quite a bit. I think about this. Finally I say, 'So do you, Kate.' We smile at each other. And Victor.

'We have to take the skull back,' says Kate. 'Before we get caught.'

I stare up at the skull.

Take me back where I belong, mate, says Major Manners.

I don't tell Kate that Major Manners can talk to me. She'll think I am crazy.

'The only trouble is,' I say out loud, 'someone has put the concrete block back and we'll never be strong enough to lift it off.'

'You could just bury him here in the sand,' she says. 'No one would know.'

I would, says Major Manners.

'I would,' I say.

'I would,' says Victor. I peer into his eyes. His words are not an echo. He takes the broom from my hand.

I look up at the sky. There is a cloud that looks like a smiling face. 'Let's go . . . mate,' I say to Victor.

Without another word we jump to our feet and start to walk along the deserted beach towards the grave.

We must look strange. Three children carrying a bony head on a broom handle, one of them a great big student from Billabong who is not as clever as the small girl who holds his hand. I wonder what all the others would think: Ian Douglas and his tough mates, Rev Carpenter who made me repeat his words, Stinker the cruel teacher, my father who can't bring himself to tell me how babies get started and my mother who has never kissed or hugged me. What would they all think of us?

'We are weird,' I say to myself.

No mate, says Major Manners. ***They** are weird*.

The waves race up and down the sand and nip at

our feet like liquid fingers. The sky stretches above us. A high wind is tearing the smiling face in the cloud to pieces. Now it looks like an angry devil. I suddenly shiver. It's not a good sign.

23

a grave situation

AFTER A LONG, tiring walk we reach the track that leads up into the sand dunes. We make our way up towards the grave which is still out of sight.

I hear voices.

We are not alone.

Oh no. Are the Police waiting for us? Is it Ian Douglas and his mob? It can't be because it is school time. The kids at my school will all be safely out in the playground eating sandwiches. I look at my watch – a Timex with luminous hands and a leather strap. I am lucky because there are only three children in our grade with a watch and I am one of them. Sometimes at night when I am in bed I stare at the green glowing pointers as they shine in the dark. Towards midnight they start to fade and finally disappear altogether. It's as if the luminous hands save up the sunshine but it gradually gets used up. Like life. One day all of my life will be used up. I will be just a skull and bones like Major Manners.

I slap my own head. This is no time for daydreaming. There is someone up near the grave.

A voice floats loudly on the air above the sound of the crashing waves.

'Bloody, bloody, bloody.'

I have heard that voice before.

Randolph, the Seagull Boy.

'Sh . . .' I say to Kate and Victor.

But Victor knows who owns that voice too. He waves the broom around and makes Major Manners rattle as he climbs up the sand dune.

'Bloody, bloody, bloody,' shouts Victor.

'No, no, no,' I yell.

'Yes, yes, yes,' yells Victor.

Victor disappears over the top of the dune. I have no choice but to follow. Kate comes after me with fearless steps.

There are about ten Billabong kids on the other side of the fence. But they're not going to be there for much longer. Richard has a large pair of wire cutters and he is snipping away at the hole in the fence. It was probably him who cut the hole in the first place. It must have been the Billabong students, not Ian Douglas and the gang, who lifted the top off the grave, punched a hole in the coffin, and took out the skull. They would have run for it when Mr Hooper or another teacher came by or the school bell rang.

The Billabong students see Victor holding the skull and start to yell and whoop. Some are scared and race off but most of them go crazy with excitement. Victor prances up and down in front of the fence waving the skull like a Vandal general in front of his victorious troops.

Richard makes the last snip with his strong hands and removes a circle of wire. He dives through the hole and one by one the rest of the Billabong students follow him to our side of the fence. They form a circle and dance around Victor and his skull. I have to put a stop to this. I have to put Major Manners back in his coffin before we are discovered.

I try to take the broom from Victor's hands but he doesn't want to give it up.

'Please,' I say.

This doesn't work. 'Please' has no effect. Victor holds the broom behind his back.

'Can I have it, please, Victor?' says Kate.

Victor pauses, thinks about this then shakes his head. Even for Kate he won't hand over the skull.

I start waving my hands around trying to make the excited mob listen. I shout at them but that doesn't work either.

'This is Major Manners,' I yell, pointing to the top of Victor's broom handle. 'A brave soldier who defended his country in the War. A mighty warrior.'

Some of them are looking up at the skull with puzzled expressions. They don't seem to connect it with a live person.

'Bloody,' says Randolph.

'Yes,' I yell. 'Bloody good man. He must be returned to his grave. You shouldn't have taken him out of the coffin.'

Richard and a few others start mumbling crossly under their breath when I say this. Russell is shaking his huge head. Victor looks at his toes like a small child caught pinching food from the fridge.

'You should've left him in there. But it's not too late. We can put him back now and no one will know.'

My speech gets only blank looks. No one seems to understand. I must have used too many long words.

Major Manners stares down from the top of the broom as Kate walks over to the grave and bends down. She makes out that she is trying to lift the concrete block. Her face goes red and she makes a little groaning noise.

Richard rushes to her side and tries to lift the slab with her. Even with his help she can't do it.

I go to the other side of the grave and grab the slab with both hands.

There is a pause. All the boys look at each other. Then they hurry to the concrete block and surround it. One by one they bend down and grab the edge.

'Lift,' I grunt.

'Lift,' comes back the chorus.

Victor holds the skull up high. 'Lift,' he yells.

'Lift,' comes back the chorus.

It reminds me of a Roman galleon with the slave master yelling out 'row' and all the slaves echoing his words with every stroke. Victor is leading the way. Everyone is repeating *his* words now.

'Lift,' shouts Victor. He is enjoying the power of words.

'Lift,' comes the reply.

We all struggle. Eyes bulge. Veins stand out on foreheads. Sweat pours down faces. But the slab does not move.

'Lift,' urges Victor.

This time there is no reply. But there is a movement.

The grave cover moves. We have it a few inches off the ground. My back is killing me. Up, up, up.

We are standing.

We have it.

24

beneath a bone

THE BILLABONG STUDENTS and Kate and I have managed to lift the concrete top off the grave. But now what? I am worried that someone will slip into the hole. Richard, who is at the end, is in danger of falling in.

'Over here,' I shout.

Richard edges his way around to my side and we all stagger towards the sand dune which cuts us off from the sea. At last we are clear of the grave. We inch our way forward with the concrete block held between us.

'Stop now,' I say.

Each of us stands there like a weight-lifter who has

the barbell up to his waist but doesn't know how to put it down.

'Get your toes out of the way,' I scream.

There is a shuffle as they all do what I say. I go to speak but there is a bit of sand in my throat and all I can do is cough.

'Let go,' yells Kate.

Everyone lets go at the sound of her voice. The concrete slab lands with an almighty thump.

The Billabong boys all fall to the ground and make exaggerated noises of exhaustion. They are having fun.

'I'm knackered.'

'Puffed out.'

'Stuffed.'

'Bloody heavy.'

There is much laughing and puffing and holding of sides.

Suddenly a bell sounds. It is the Billabong end-of-lunch bell calling the pupils back to class. Richard dives back through the hole. The others follow.

'Don't tell anyone about this,' I yell.

'They won't,' says Kate. 'They don't want to get into trouble for climbing through the fence.'

In a flash they have gone. All of them. Except Victor.

'You'd better go too, Victor,' says Kate.

'Give me the skull, Victor,' I say.

Victor just shakes his head. He is very stubborn sometimes, is Victor. The three of us stare down into the grave at the coffin below.

'There's no ladder,' says Kate. 'How will we get down?'

She's right. Whoever put the slab back must have taken the ladder. We won't be able to put Major Manners' head back inside his coffin unless I can get down there somehow. If I jump into the grave I won't be able to climb out.

There are the remains of rotting boards on the sides but they are no stronger than dry cardboard. Most have gone altogether leaving the sandy walls without support. Already some parts have fallen in.

'We'll just have to throw him back down,' I say. 'Maybe the Police or Mr Hooper will see and finish the job.'

'No,' screams Victor.

He doesn't want us to put the skull in the grave. He thinks we are trying to bury a friend. I grab the broom handle and pull. Victor pulls back and the broom begins to shake like crazy. Suddenly the skull falls. It lands heavily on the sand. I dive for it but Victor is too quick. He grabs the skull with two hands. So do I.

Victor tugs. I hang on firmly. Kate rushes over to help. She grabs me around the waist and tries to drag me and the skull away from Victor.

'Stop it,' I shout. 'You'll break it.'

'Let go, Victor,' orders Kate.

Victor does not do what Kate says. He will not let go. He pulls even harder. So do I. Suddenly Victor loses his grip. Kate and I go flying backwards.

Into the grave.

We fall screaming down into the hole and land with a thud on the sand to one side of the coffin. A huge landslide of sand pours down and partly buries us. We are both winded and fight for breath. Sand continues to fall.

'Stand up, stand up,' I yell at Kate. 'Before we're buried.'

We struggle to our feet and I don't even notice that every bone in my body is aching. The skull is lying on the other side of the coffin.

'Help,' Kate yells up at the sky above.

'Help,' I scream at Major Manners.

I can't, mate, he says. *It's up to you.*

Even though I am in such danger, my mind rushes off on its own track. All this is about returning Major Manners to his grave. Even if it is our grave too, I will snatch a second or two to put him back where he belongs. I grab the skull and place it over the hole in the lead coffin. I push downwards.

'What are you doing?' yells Kate. 'We have to get out of here.'

'It won't fit,' I groan.

It won't either. The hole is too small. The skull will just not go back through the opening no matter how hard I push.

Whoomph. More sand falls. I have to free my hands and get out of here before we are buried. I shove the skull into a small ledge which has formed behind a decayed board at the end of the grave.

I look up at Victor who is peering down at us with wild eyes. He is our only hope. He is kind. He is innocent. But he's not smart.

'It's up to you and me, Victor,' I call out. 'No one else is here. We have to get Kate out.'

'And you,' says Kate.

'You first,' I say. 'I can lift you but you can't lift me. You can go and get help.'

'Help us, Victor,' I call.

Victor pushes a hand into his pocket. He pulls out a handful of boiled lollies and begins throwing them down at Kate. They rain down on us just as they did on me when I was in the grave last time.

'Don't,' I yell. 'Don't.'

Victor's face falls. He is only trying to help. The poor kid doesn't understand what is going on. He points down to the skull.

'Mine,' says Victor. 'Friend.' He wants Major Manners back.

Whoomph. Another sandfall. This time it dumps around both of us and we are buried up to our knees. Oh, no, no, no. Now we will both be drowned in sand. How can I possibly get Kate out? I give it everything I've got and manage to lean towards her, reaching forward. I begin digging away the sand from around her like a dog uncovering a bone. Finally she manages to release her legs from the grip of the sand.

'Kate,' I say. 'Jump on to my shoulders. Reach up and grab Victor's hand. Don't be scared.'

'I'm not scared,' she says with a trembling voice.

Kate scrambles onto my shoulders. She sits there like a little girl on her father's shoulders.

'Reach up, Kate,' I say.

She stretches up her arms but Victor simply looks down. He doesn't do anything to help. I can see he is looking at the skull.

'Stretch,' I yell. 'Stretch.'

Kate stretches but still Victor does nothing but look. All he wants is the skull. He hangs over the edge of the grave and dangles one arm down, trying to reach it. More sand falls. My shoulders start to ache. Kate is too heavy and too far away from Victor.

'I'm going to push you up,' I grunt. 'You have to stand up.'

Kate squirms around desperately.

'Hurry,' I say.

'I'm trying, I'm trying,' she gasps.

It is tough going but finally I push Kate up until she is kneeling on my shoulders. She jiggles around a bit and with me holding her hands manages to move to a squatting position. Then, with shaking knees, she stands with her shoes right next to my ears and steadies herself against the edge of the grave with one hand. The wall around her hand begins to collapse and sand pours down around us.

'Climb up,' I yell.

Kate stretches but there are still no hands to meet hers.

The skull is still lodged in the little hollow just above my face.

My strength is giving out. I can't last much longer. With one hand on Kate's ankle, I reach across with my other hand and snatch the skull. 'Here, grab the skull,' I groan to Kate.

'Why?'

'Grab it, quick. And give it to Victor.'

She doesn't seem to know what I have in mind but she grabs the skull by putting one hand through the hole in the back of the skull and gripping the ridge between the eyes with her fingers.

'Give it to Victor,' I yell. 'And don't let go.'

Victor's eyes light up. He sees the skull in Kate's trembling hand. He grabs it with two hands and pulls. He really wants that skull. He is strong but his fingers are stubby. The weight on my shoulders grows lighter. Victor's face is red and straining. He is lifting the skull upwards and Kate with it. But he is flat on his stomach and I can see that he can't pull her weight backwards.

I put my hands under her feet and shove.

I push Kate up a few more inches and she manages to grasp the back of Victor's shirt. With a grunt she drags herself onto his back. Suddenly she has gone. Victor has wriggled back, taking Kate and the skull with him. She's safe.

My relief turns to panic. The edges of the grave are collapsing all around me. The sand is pouring down like dry rain. I try and try and eventually manage to pull out one leg and then the other. I stand on the fallen sand but my face is still about the length of my arm below the top of the grave. Suddenly there is an enormous collapse of sand. I do my desperate dance trying to stop my legs from being buried. I manage to stay on top of the sand until my face is about a foot below the surface. There is another enormous collapse. The sand falls too quickly. It covers my waist. It is up to my chest. It covers my shoulders and then my neck. I am just a head poking out the bottom of a shallow hole. Sand is running down the edges onto my chin.

I take a deep gasp of air and then – the greedy sand covers my mouth. And my nose. Oh, merciful Heaven. Help. I can't breathe.

Victor is prancing around holding the skull. He doesn't understand that I am suffocating. I can't talk. I can't scream out my fear. I have no voice. Only my eyes and the top of my head are above ground and soon they will be covered too.

The sand is running slowly down the edges of the hole on to my face like honey tipped from a jar. Grains of sand scratch my eyes. Kate falls to her knees above me and begins digging as fast as she can. She uncovers my nose and mouth and I spit out dry sand and begin to cough.

'Go for help,' I splutter. 'There might be someone on the beach.'

The deadly flow is still drifting down despite Kate's efforts to pull me up. She begins to dig. But it is hopeless.

'I don't want to leave you,' she sobs. 'But I can't stop the sand.'

I know this is true. Hands are such small shovels.

'Victor will help me. Go,' I shriek.

Kate's eyes are filled with doubt. But she jumps to her feet. And is gone.

'Help me, Victor,' I yell.

Victor just dances around with the skull. He is so happy to have it back.

I have to think. Think, think, think. I am going to suffocate. If there was a bucket or a tin Victor could put it over my head to give me a breathing hole.

'Put the skull over my face,' I yell at Victor. 'To keep the sand out.'

Victor hugs the skull to himself and takes a step backwards. I can see that he is about to run. The sand is trickling down over my chin again. These are my last moments.

'Victor,' I say. 'You are my friend. Help me please. Put the skull on my face. I will die if you don't.'

Victor seems to be thinking this over, like a judge deciding whether a prisoner is guilty or innocent. Finally he decides in my favour. He bends down and places the hole in the back of the skull over my face. Just in time. My mouth and eyes and nose are completely inside the round brain-box. The sand continues to pour around the base of the skull. Now I have two heads.

The sand can't reach my face. I am safe for a second or two. Victor kneels down and stares in through the bony eye holes.

'Go for help,' I say. 'Please, Victor. Get help.'

'Yes . . .' He is struggling to say something. '. . . Hedley.'

Victor vanishes. I am alone. Buried beneath a bone.

25

dead man talking

IT IS SILENT in my grave. Major Manners says nothing. I am standing buried in sand.

The skull keeps me alive by allowing me to breathe through the remains of Major Manners' head. Two pairs of eyes stare up from the sand. His are empty but mine gaze up through his sockets. My mouth and eyes are lined with sand and grit. I try not to move as the slightest vibration may bring more sand drifting into the skull to block my airway.

I can see the blue sky through the eye sockets. But to anyone above I am no more than a half-buried skull peering up from the sand. I am invisible.

Time passes slowly. The weight of the sand around my chest makes it difficult to breathe. I feel faint. It's like being encased in concrete. Think, think, think. Don't faint. Don't fall into that dark night. Once you are there, that's it. There is no returning.

Think about anything. Anything at all.

My thoughts wander off as if I have no part in where they go.

All right, how much pee *do* you put in to make a baby? Why is that so funny? Use your brains, Hedley. Put two and two together and get . . . Four.

All of a sudden a light bulb goes on in my head. I realise why they were all laughing at me. I have been so dumb. Of course. You fool, Hopkins. You do not put *any* pee in. It's not pee at all. I have remembered what happened to me when I hugged my pillow. When I was thinking about the twelve dancing ladies.

That sticky white stuff that came out of my stiffy . . . that's what makes babies.

Even though I am buried and about to die, I still feel enormous relief. I have not caught some terrible disease. God is not punishing me. I bet every other boy has the same thing happen to him. They probably think about naked ladies too. Probably every boy in the country dreams about twelve dancing ladies. They probably all hug their pillows and have wicked thoughts.

Like me.

I am normal.

Hooray.

Suddenly life seems good. I don't want to die buried beneath the sand. Someone please come and save me.

What's that? I feel a faint tremor above me and then another. Like silent drumbeats seeping through the dunes. Footsteps. Someone is coming.

Kate?

Victor?

Mr Hooper from Billabong?

'Gently, gently,' I pray. I pray very hard. 'Don't disturb the sand. Don't choke off my air.'

Voices. Muffled. I have heard them before. My stomach lurches. All my happy feelings vanish.

A voice speaks.

'It's filled in. Some fool has filled in the grave.'

'Shit.'

'If that little Pommie Headless Hopkins put the skull back, it's all over. We'll never get it now.'

My heart pounds louder than ever. It is Ian Douglas, Frank Kelly and Henderson. Mouse isn't with them. They have come for the skull. Will they see it? Do I want them to see it? A leg comes into view and a sprinkling of sand showers down through Major Manners' nose holes. Please don't step on me, I pray again. Please don't drown me in sand.

The leg disappears. What if they just grab the skull and run? I will die. What if they see me here? Will they leave me to perish? No, never. Even mean kids like Ian Douglas and his gang wouldn't do that. They aren't criminals. They wouldn't let me choke to death in sand. They'll dig me out. They will, they will. They must, they must.

They might, they might . . .

But they will keep the skull, that's for sure.

Never mind that. I want to live. Badly.

I decide to call for help. It's my only chance. More sand trickles down. My mouth is so dry that I have trouble spitting it out. I try to say 'help' but all I can manage is a choked cry. A long, hopeless wailing cry of despair.

The voices above fall silent. Three heads stare down.

Silence. But only for a few seconds.

'Aaagh,' the three heads scream. 'Aaagh.'

The three heads vanish.

Vibrations through the sand again. Pounding. Foot-steps fleeing into the dunes.

They didn't see *me*. They saw the skull. Staring up from a grave. They heard it cry out.

They heard a dead man talking.

Even though I am about to die, I start to laugh.

My cackling voice from the grave erupts from Major Manners' mouth. His whole head shakes with mirth. Handfuls of sand pour down through the skull's eye sockets on to my face.

The world turns black.

I am dead.

26

angels

LAUGHTER, LAUGHTER. THAT'S all I hear. Crazy laughter. Mad laughter. I have taken my joke of a life into the next world. The angels are chuckling with me. They are staring down with big grins. But they are weird-looking angels. Not what I expected. One of them is bald. One has no teeth. One has a runny nose. Another stands on one leg yelling out 'bloody' at the top of his voice. One of them is Victor. He shoves a boiled lolly into my mouth. A gobstopper. It is covered in sand and makes me choke. I see angels but I am not in Heaven. And I am not in Hell.

The smallest one of all bends down and smiles.

'I went into Billabong,' says Kate. 'And got Mr Hooper.'

I am lying on the sand surrounded by the boys from Billabong. There are fifteen of them. Mr Hooper has brought his class and they have dug me out. I have been saved by a class of, of . . . kids. They have saved me. They prance and dance and shout. Victor has Major Manners tucked under his arm. He is so happy.

I am so happy.

I jump up and kiss Victor on the cheek. Victor kisses Major Manners. Suddenly everyone starts to kiss each other. They think it is so funny. Like ancient people in front of a crackling camp fire, they dance around the collapsed grave. The Billabong boys stand on their hands. They jump and laugh and shout. I am too weary to join in but I hug Mr Hooper – a teacher – I actually hug a teacher. And then I hug Kate.

The word 'bloody' rings out every now and then. In the end the pace starts to slow. They are all exhausted. They fall to the ground complaining good-naturedly.

'I'm knackered.'

'Puffed out.'

'Stuffed.'

There is much laughing and puffing and holding of sides.

Above us the bright sun smiles at the joke.

Inside I am laughing. I'm feeling so good. For once in my life I have come out on top.

Somewhere in the distance Ian Douglas and his mates will be puffed out too. I bet they have run to the Police Station and are trying to get enough breath to explain that they have heard a voice from the grave. They are going to feel so silly when they find out.

That it was only me.

27

who did it?

KATE AND I are happy as we walk over the sand dunes. We are happy as we splash along the beach. We are happy making our way along the pavement towards home. But we are not happy when we get to our street and see what lies ahead.

'What sort of car does Mr Hooper have?' says Kate.

I stare at the black FX Holden parked outside our house. All my warm feelings disappear like water running down a plughole.

'Not one with POLICE written on the side,' I say. 'We're really in for it now.'

For a second I think about running away. But I don't. Mum and Dad are standing there with a policeman and they don't look too pleased.

'Quick, get the sand off,' says Kate.

She starts to stamp her shoes on the footpath to remove the sand which clearly tells the story of where we have been.

Mum spots us. 'Here they are,' she shouts in a relieved voice. She hurries down the street, grabs Kate with one hand and me with the other, and drags us quickly back to where Dad and the policeman are waiting.

Mum bends down and whispers urgently. 'Pull up your socks,' she says. 'You are in big trouble.'

I let go of Mum's hand and bend down to pull up my socks. Mum sees the back of my legs. 'How did that happen?' she asks.

Before I can answer, the policeman asks a question of his own.

'Did you rob that grave, Hopkins?' he says. 'Did you help steal a skull?'

What can I say? It's true. I open my mouth to speak but Dad cuts me off.

'Don't answer,' he says firmly.

The policeman doesn't seem pleased. 'I think we had better go to the Police Station,' he says. 'We have a few other vandals down there as well.'

'By all means,' says Dad. 'Let's sort this out once and for all. We may want to call a solicitor.'

Normally it would be great riding in a police car. But I hardly notice what's happening. Dad's in the front and I am between Kate and Mum in the back. I suppose I'm in the middle so that I can't make a run for it. I just feel terrible. This is not the happy ending I wanted. The way it is going I will end up in prison. Mum hisses in my ear wanting to know all sorts of things about what's happened but I hardly know what I am saying as I answer her. All I can think about is vandals and dunny men and people being horsewhipped.

And a cold, damp prison cell.

In no time we are in an office at the Police Station. Mr Hooper is there and for a few seconds I feel a bit better. He nods to me and forces a smile. Behind a desk is a different policeman named Sergeant Clifford. He is tall and strong and has a stern expression. The feeling of doom returns. This is not looking good.

Ian Douglas is here with his father who seems angry. I know who he is because he is on the vestry at church with Dad. Henderson and Frank Kelly are sitting with them trying to appear innocent. Mouse isn't here. Sergeant Clifford points to empty chairs and we all sit down.

'I don't know what Ian and his friends are here for,' says Mr Douglas sharply. 'All they have done is report a crime.' He turns and frowns at me. 'But *this* lad has broken into a grave and vandalised it.'

I gasp loudly. This is so unfair. I want to scream out *liar*. But I would need a million words to tell the whole story. Not just one. And no one would believe me anyway.

'That's right,' says Ian Douglas. 'Hopkins did it.'

'Quiet, if you don't mind,' growls Sergeant Clifford. 'I'll do all the talking for the present.'

'No, you won't,' Mr Hooper cuts in. 'You came to Billabong and took my boys. I want them back.'

'Your boys are a menace,' says Sergeant Clifford. 'They are in a cell down below.'

Ian Douglas and his mates try not to look smug at this news. Kate frowns.

'On what charge?' says Mr Hooper angrily.

Sergeant Clifford's eyes narrow. 'They are a danger to the community,' he says. 'They're crazy. They are locked up for the public good. One of them won't stop swearing. And the bald one just repeats everything you say.'

A cold shiver of despair runs from my head to my toes. Victor must be terrified in a damp dark cell. Now he has gone back to his echo way of talking.

Sergeant Clifford taps a large square tin which sits on his desk. On the side is a label saying ARNOTT'S BISCUITS. Underneath someone has written: STAFF ONLY – NOT TO BE GIVEN TO PRISONERS. For a second I think Sergeant Clifford is going to offer us refreshments.

But instead he says, 'It was the bald one who stole the skull. My officers caught him red-handed.'

I realise with a shock that Major Manners' head is inside the biscuit tin. Victor must have run off with the head and got caught.

'Not so,' says Mr Hooper. 'I tried to tell you earlier. My boys didn't do it.'

'I think you'll find I'm right,' says Sergeant Clifford. 'But whoever it was that did do it, could well end up in a reformatory. A prison for wayward youths.'

I can't help thinking he is saying all this especially for my benefit. Mum and Dad are alarmed. I am scared.

Mr Hooper has other things on his mind. 'Bring my boys up here,' he says firmly. 'They're only children.'

'They won't understand a thing,' says Sergeant Clifford.

'They have a right to be heard,' says Mr Hooper. 'I'm not saying another word until they're released.'

There is a long silence.

Sergeant Clifford stands and leaves the room. Mr

Hooper gives me a small smile. The gang nudge each other knowing they have nothing to worry about.

I wonder what it is like in a reformatory.

After a bit I hear a familiar sound.

'Bloody, bloody, bloody.'

Sergeant Clifford comes in pulling Michael behind him in his cut-down pram. Victor, Russell, Randolph and Richard follow silently. Michael and Russell have tears in their eyes. Richard's nose is running. They are a sorry lot and they rush over to Mr Hooper's side like lost infants finding their mother.

'It's okay, boys,' says Mr Hooper gently. 'Nothing is going to happen to you. I promise.'

There is a bit of snuffling but the Billabong boys settle down.

'These are the culprits,' says Sergeant Clifford. 'These retarded people opened up the coffin and took out the skull. Hedley Hopkins here and the other normal boys tried to talk them out of it. Hedley got half-buried in the sand trying to stop them. He was lucky to get off with his life.'

Dad starts nodding. 'That's right,' he says. 'They are not too bright. They didn't know what they were doing.'

Sergeant Clifford talks to Victor. 'I know you are involved in this,' he says. 'We caught you running down the street with the skull. We know you vandalised the grave. Own up, boy.'

Victor says nothing but he looks around with frightened eyes.

'Own up,' says Sergeant Clifford crossly. 'Just tell us the truth and it will all be over. It's simple, boy. Say the words – I . . . did . . . it.'

Oh no.

Victor doesn't hesitate. 'I did it,' he echoes.

Sergeant Clifford smiles grimly.

'Yeah,' says Ian Douglas. 'It was the loonies.'

The room falls silent again. This explanation seems to suit everyone.

Except Mr Hooper. He does not look pleased at all.

And the Billabong boys are confused.

Randolph stands on one leg. 'Bloody, bloody, bloody,' he says.

Michael is rocking in his pram like a baby. He is dribbling a bit and just keeps saying the one word. 'Didn't, didn't, didn't.'

Russell shakes his enormous head with a puzzled look. It's as if he is trying to find some words inside there that have become lost.

Richard wears a guilty expression.

'You were all in it, weren't you?' Sergeant Clifford says to Richard. 'What was your part in this?'

'Cut the wire,' Richard mumbles.

'Ah ha,' says Sergeant Clifford. Now he is certain that he knows the truth. He reminds me of Miss Marple, the detective in a book, when she has cracked a case.

I am ashamed about letting the Billabong boys take the blame. But I am too scared to own up. I don't want to go to a reformatory.

'As I said, these boys are retarded and don't know any better,' says Sergeant Clifford. 'They have no place with normal people.'

Mr Hooper keeps looking at me as if he is expecting me to say something. He is probably thinking there is no way Victor can go to our school now.

I feel terrible.

The whole thing is my fault.

I take a deep breath.

'This is all wrong,' I say. '*I* took the skull.'

28

blue heaven

EVERYONE TURNS TO look at me. They gasp.

'Told ya,' yells Ian Douglas. 'We never went near it. Headless stole the skull.'

'Yeah, that's right,' say Henderson and Kelly.

Now I'm well and truly on the hook. Dad and Mum are worried. Mr Hooper is looking at me with sad approval.

'Careful, lad,' says Sergeant Clifford. 'We may not want to hear this. Think before you say any more.'

I do think. But not for long.

'The kids from Billabong are heroes,' I say. 'They saved my life. I would be dead if it wasn't for them.'

'Me too,' says Kate. 'Victor saved us.'

'Victor saved us,' says Victor.

'Heroes,' says Russell proudly.

'Bloody, bloody, bloody,' says Randolph.

'This is what really happened,' I say quickly. 'Kate and I found the grave with the skull already in the bottom where someone had broken in and taken it out of the coffin and Ian Douglas and his gang dared me to get it and if I did they would let me join the gang so . . .'

My story is blurping out in one long rush. Ian Douglas and his friends are shaking their heads as if all this is untrue but I don't let that stop me. I take in another huge breath and the words pour out like monkeys escaping from a cage.

'. . . I got the ladder where they told me it was kept and went and took the skull but Major Manners was sad so I went to put his skull back but Kate and I fell in and the Billabong children saved us when the walls caved in.'

I have said it.

I have told the truth.

I have stepped off the diving board.

'It's true,' says Kate. 'They saved our lives.'

Mum is staring at the Billabong boys in shocked appreciation.

Sergeant Clifford fiddles with a pair of handcuffs

and frowns at me as if I am Jack the Ripper. I am the guilty one. I have confessed and now I will have to pay the price. My life is over. I expect the reformatory will be full of kids like Ian Douglas.

'Who on earth is Major Manners?' says Dad.

'*He* is,' I say pointing to the biscuit tin on the desk.

'The Hopkins kid is nuts too,' says Ian Douglas's father. 'And anyway, my boy didn't have a ladder.'

'He did,' I shout hopelessly. I am all choked up and can hardly get the words out. 'They hid it under the pier. And . . .'

Sergeant Clifford interrupts. 'If this is all true,' he says. 'Who took the skull out of the coffin in the first place? All we are getting here is lies. One little detail ruins your whole story, Hedley Hopkins. If it wasn't you, who was it? I bet you can't answer that one.'

He is right. I can't. Maybe Victor did break into the coffin. Or it could have been Ian Douglas. Kate and I both turn in his direction.

'Don't look at us,' yells Ian Douglas. 'The whole thing was already broken open and a ladder was there. Someone was coming so we pinched the ladder and raced off with it. But that's all we did. Headless is lying. He busted open the coffin before we got there. Or one of the loonies did.'

'They are not loonies,' says Mum. 'They saved my children's lives.'

Everyone is quiet. We will probably never find out who vandalised the coffin. Everyone will always think that I did it even though I didn't.

'I did not punch the hole in the coffin,' I say. 'Cross my heart and hope to die.'

Every eye looks at me. I can see doubt in nearly all of them.

'Who did do it then?' repeats Sergeant Clifford. 'Who made the hole in the coffin? Come on. Own up.'

No one speaks.

I hear Sergeant Clifford's clock ticking on the wall. I hear my own blood pulsing in my ears.

And I hear a firm and gentle voice saying something amazing.

'I did. I made the hole in the coffin.'

I can't believe this. It's Mr Hooper.

'But I didn't take out the skull,' he says. 'I made the hole so I could put the head back. Back in the coffin with the rest of the skeleton. Then I looked up and saw my boys staring down at me. They should have been in bed so I left the skull in the grave and took them home through the gap in the fence. When I returned, my ladder was gone and I couldn't get down inside the grave. I decided I would come back to finish the job later.'

Kate looks as if she is trying to solve a very hard sum at school. Like the rest of us, she can't quite follow it all. I am so relieved that the truth is out. But Mr Hooper the vandal? Surely not.

Mr Hooper continues. 'To my horror, when I returned, the skull was gone,' he says.

Sergeant Clifford doesn't believe him. 'Why wasn't the skull in the coffin then?' he says. 'Who took it out in the first place? Was it you?'

'I just told you I didn't,' says Mr Hooper. 'It was never in there at all. That grave was the resting place of Mighty Manny, the escaped convict.'

I am stunned. A convict. Not a soldier.

Mr Douglas draws in breath noisily. 'Mad Dog Manny,' he gasps. 'A criminal. Deported from England on a convict ship.'

'For spitting on the footpath,' says Mr Hooper, angrily.

'Escaped. Ran off and lived with the Abos,' says Mr Douglas.

'A *convict*,' I say under my breath. 'I thought Major Manners was a hero.'

Mr Hooper hears my whisper. 'Mighty Manny *was* a hero,' he says firmly. 'He escaped into the wild bushland in bare feet. Walked over a thousand miles to this very place to get away from the soldiers. Arrived half dead. The Aboriginal people took him in. Life was good by the sea with plenty of fish and game. He married and had children.'

'A lubra and little black kids,' says Mr Douglas scornfully.

'His *wife and children*,' Mr Hooper says. 'He lived here with his *family*.'

I can see Mr Hooper is getting very upset.

Mr Douglas looks puzzled. Finally he says, 'Well, he was still an escaped convict and lived with savages so he got what he deserved.'

'He was murdered by settlers who wanted the land,' says Mr Hooper. 'He didn't deserve that. He died protecting his people. My people.'

'Your people?' says an amazed Mr Douglas.

'Yes, *my* people. Mighty Manny was my great-grandfather. And his Aboriginal wife was my great-grandmother. Thirty settlers with guns attacked Manny and twelve Aborigines around their camp fire. The women and children fled into the bush. The men fought back, but in the end they were all killed. Guns against spears. My people had no hope.'

Mr Hooper pauses. I can see that he is about to say something terrible. He has tears in his eyes. Everyone is waiting.

'The *settlers* were the savages, Mr Douglas.'

'How so?' spits out Mr Douglas.

We all wait for the answer.

'They took the men's heads for trophies – including Manny's. Those settlers were head-hunters.'

'That's shocking,' says Mum. She is upset. Her lips are quivering.

I give a shudder. Poor, poor Major Manners.

'Okay, okay,' says Sergeant Clifford. 'I can see how you feel, Mr Hooper. But where is all this going?' He taps the biscuit tin on his desk.

Mr Hooper rushes on with his story.

'After the . . . murder of my ancestors, a missionary, the Rev Thatcher who was just out from England on a sailing ship, paid for Manny's coffin and the grave for his body. But his skull was never found.'

'Until you came along,' says Sergeant Clifford.

'That's right,' says Mr Hooper. He is getting really worked up now. 'I've been looking for Manny's head all my life. I finally found it in a tiny private museum near Woods Point in the mountains. It was on a shelf next to the stuffed remains of a rabbit with five legs. I paid a thousand pounds for it. Now Mighty Manny's head must go back where it belongs,' he finishes.

Nobody knows what to say.

It's time for me to speak up again.

'A person's head and body *should* be together,' I say. 'What was done was wrong.'

'It's a good point, son,' says Dad.

'A *very* good point,' Mum adds.

'And I was right all along,' I say. 'I knew it. The skull belonged to a brave man. A man defending his people. I'm glad Maj . . . er, Mighty Manny is going back where he belongs. He can rest in peace now. I'm sorry I took his skull.'

Thanks, mate, says a voice in my head. The voice of my old friend. Somehow I think this is the last time he will talk to me. And me to him.

Mr Douglas scrambles to his feet.

'You don't need us any more, Sergeant,' he says. 'We're leaving.'

'I think that would be a good idea,' says Dad.

Mr Douglas heads for the door followed by the gang. Sergeant Clifford nods his permission.

My father turns to Sergeant Clifford and clears his throat.

'Hedley was *returning* the skull,' he says. 'That must count in his favour.'

'Indeed,' says Mum. 'He is a kind boy. He was chosen to help out at Billabong.'

Before Sergeant Clifford can say anything, Dad gets up and shakes Victor's hand.

'I want to thank you boys for saving Hedley and Kate's lives,' he says. 'A wonderful effort. Brave and smart. Great work.'

Dad takes each of the boys' hands. He thanks every one of them. Kate follows him along. She shakes every hand too. So do I. And so does Mum. The Billabong boys are happy and embarrassed at the same time. They are so proud of themselves.

'Didn't, didn't, didn't do much,' says Michael.

'Dug him out,' says Richard.

'Bloody knackered,' says Randolph.

'Sergeant,' says Mr Hooper. 'It was a long time ago. But I don't believe that Manny's murderers were ever charged. Or punished. The men who stole his skull in the first place are the guilty ones. Not this innocent boy. Nor the kids from Billabong.'

Sergeant Clifford regards me with a serious expression. Then he looks at the poor boys from Billabong. They seem so scared and harmless and I can see he is moved by the scene he's just witnessed. Finally he makes an announcement in a slow, kindly voice.

'The best course of action might be to forget the whole thing,' he says. 'After all, no one has been hurt.'

'It's the best for everyone,' says Mum. 'Thank you.'

'You're a good man, Sergeant,' says Dad.

Sergeant Clifford tries to hide a smile.

Oh, wow. Now I'm off the hook. I can't believe it. What a relief. Kate digs me in the ribs. She is happy and so am I. Very happy indeed.

There is a shuffling of feet. Everyone seems to want to get out of here now. I do, that's for sure. Before Sergeant Clifford changes his mind.

Victor marches over to the biscuit tin on the desk. He taps it with one finger.

'Bloody good bloke,' he says.

Mr Hooper and I exchange looks. We break into enormous knowing smiles and Mr Hooper gently takes the biscuit tin from Victor's hands.

'I think this is mine,' he says.

We know that although he is looking at Victor, Mr Hooper is really talking to Sergeant Clifford.

'Well, Mr Hooper, it's a little late to open a murder investigation into his death,' he says. 'So I guess Mighty Manny is yours to bury.'

'Let's go, boys,' says Mr Hooper. 'I think I need a nice cold lime milkshake.'

'Me too,' yells Michael. 'Me too.'

The boys rush over to Mr Hooper. Richard pats him on the back. They are happiest of all about the thought of a milkshake.

'Banana?' yells Richard.

'No, strawberry,' shouts Michael.

The boys disappear through the door after Mr Hooper. The sound of their loud voices can be heard even through the walls of the Police Station.

'Blue heaven,' I hear Victor call out from the pavement outside.

It's funny but somehow or other the boys' voices calling out their favourite flavours seem like a victory. Almost as if they are claiming the streets.

'Well,' says Sergeant Clifford. 'I wouldn't mind a drink myself. Now we can all go home. That's the end of that.'

'Not quite,' says Mum. She grabs me by the shoulder and turns me around so that my back faces Sergeant Clifford. Then she quickly pulls down my long socks and points to the bruises on the back of my legs.

'I want to talk about this,' she says.

29

the nougat tin

SO IT ALL turns out well. Mr Hooper gets his wish. Because Manny was married to Mr Hooper's great grandmother, the Aboriginal people hold a special burial ceremony in the sand dunes and put the skull back with the rest of the skeleton. I don't know what happened exactly because the ceremony was secret. Mr Hooper told me that some of his people dressed in possum-skin cloaks. And the smoking branch of a gum tree was waved around. No one was allowed to know more than that. It was a sacred ceremony.

I do not get into big trouble. Nor does Kate. Mum has a lot to say about me taking the skull, but hearing how I nearly died makes her less angry. Dad doesn't know what to make of it all but he is just glad that the whole thing never makes it into the newspapers. He doesn't want the family to be disgraced. And he sure doesn't want his boss to find out. So I get off with a big lecture.

Victor and the others from Billabong are heroes because they saved my life. Ian Douglas and his mates are very unpopular. No one wants to know them. Partly because they made me steal the skull and then left me to die. But also because they thought they heard a dead man talking. They are a joke. A very bad joke.

But the biggest surprise of all has to do with our teacher. For two weeks we have an emergency teacher who fills in because Stinker has gone – no one knows where. There is a rumour that he is teaching in the Correspondence School which sends out lessons by post to children who live in the outback. Some of the boys say he was sent away because he hit my legs with the strap. Who knows? I was sent home and never did hear what was said about this in Sergeant Clifford's office.

Victor does not come back to our class.

Until . . .

One day, after a couple of weeks, there he is, as large as life, sitting happily next to me in our desk.

And we have a new teacher.

'Good morning, everyone,' he says.

'Good morning, Mr Hooper,' we all chorus.

It's true. Mr Hooper is our new teacher.

'We are setting up a new program for the boys from Billabong,' he says. 'Some of them are coming here to learn with you. Starting with Victor.'

The whole class is grinning. Mr Hooper doesn't give the strap. And everyone likes him because he's a nice man.

I'm not lonely any more. Victor is my friend. So is Kate.

So is Mr Hooper. He gives me a friendly whack on the back. 'Hedley, mate,' he says. 'I want to start a special Friends of Billabong group and you are in charge.' Billabong. My blood freezes. No, not really. Just joking. 'You pick out one boy or girl to look after each new student. Every Friday they can come to Billabong and help the teachers there.'

All the kids are listening and pointing to themselves. They would like to be part of it. Friday afternoons are Dictation days. Everyone hates Dictation. Billabong would be like Heaven compared to Dictation.

The first one I choose to join the Friends of Billabong is Mouse. He's a good kid really and we become mates. It doesn't matter that I'm a Pommie. Fair dinkum, it doesn't.

Life is good.

Until . . .

One day I go home and find Mum and Dad sitting in the kitchen. On the table is a familiar-looking nougat tin. My heart stops beating. I am dead. I am history. They will know what that handkerchief was used for.

'I found this under your socks,' says Mum. She opens the tin. I can't quite understand what I am looking at. The tin is completely filled with fur.

Mum looks uncomfortable. Not angry. Almost as if she is trying to cover something up.

'Mould,' she says. 'You must have put apple cores or something in there. Mould has grown over the lot.'

I nod my head. Dad is staring at the fly that is not on the ceiling.

'Your father wants to speak to you,' says Mum. For some reason I think that she knows what's really in the tin. She puts a hand on my shoulder. It's not a hug or a kiss. But it means the same to her. As I stand to go, Mum gives me a wink.

'You know, Hedley,' she says. 'I saw something funny a few days ago. A pair of your pyjama pants up a tree in the park. A cat must have stolen them off the clothes line.'

I give an embarrassed smile.

Then I follow Dad out into the garage. He is

awkward and starts walking around touching things as if he is about to clean up but keeps changing his mind.

'Look,' he finally says. 'About that Father and Son thing. You know. Well. Don't your friends at school talk about that stuff? Gee, that's how it was done in my day.'

I think about my friends. They don't talk about things like that.

'No,' I say. 'Not really.'

'Well, look,' says Dad. 'Surely you know. You must have figured it out. Good Lord, this is embarrassing. Your mother is carrying on about it. I have to fill you in on things. But some things are private. You know. What you do in your own room. You don't talk about it. You must have worked out that's why I put a bolt on our bedroom door.'

I didn't know that but I nod. Well, at least he's not a coward.

I decide to put him out of his misery.

'I know all about it,' I say. 'I've worked it out. It's not pee.'

He looks greatly relieved.

'Good man. You figured it out. You know now, don't you? Are you sure? I don't want any more grief from your mother.'

I go over to the bench and pick up a tube of wood glue. I take off the top and squirt a little white trail on to the bench.

'Enough said, enough said,' Dad exclaims. 'Good man.' He runs out of the door.

There are two other things I find out that make me feel good. The first is about my granny. She has a dream that she is a bird. Then she finds out that you can fly to Australia on a DC3 plane. So she is coming to live with us. I am so happy. I've missed her very much. She has always been my friend.

Another good thing happens.

There is a writing competition in the *Argus* newspaper. It's for children in schools. Anyone can go in it. So I do. And for the first time ever I win something. Three pounds and a certificate to hang on the wall. A man from the *Argus* comes to our school to make the presentation. The whole school is watching. He shakes my hand. Then he opens up the story and says, 'Girls and boys. Hedley Hopkins has written a very imaginative story. I will read you just a little bit from the first page.'

Up the back I can see Mum and Dad smiling. And Kate. And Mouse. And Mr Hooper.

The man from the *Argus* begins to read:

They say there is something awful in the sand dunes.

Kate and I walk along the beach kicking seaweed and looking at stuff that has been washed up. There is not a single footprint in the sand, which means that no one has been along this way since high tide. There might be something good amongst the seaweed. So far we have only found a busted lobster pot and a dead penguin with no eyes.

It is a lonely beach with a lonely sky.

a word from paul jennings

YOU MIGHT HAVE guessed that Hedley, the boy in the story, is me. Most of this tale is true so I guess you could call it faction rather than fiction. My little sister (Ruth, not Kate) and I did discover a skull in a vandalised grave in the sand dunes. And there was a group of intellectually disabled children who suddenly popped up and frightened us. I did have a nice teacher like Mr Hooper and an awful one like Stinker, who used to hit me on the legs with a strap. When I was a young man I became a student speech therapist and one of my first clients was a boy who wouldn't speak. I gave him a jar of lollies and waited for him to ask me to undo the lid. He didn't. He ran into someone's back garden and was chased out by a dog and he really did yell, 'Dog, dog, dog.'

I did not put a skull in our fridge but I did put a dead rat in there and although my mother didn't faint she was not totally amused by it I can tell you. All the embarrassing bits about the Facts of Life and the Father and Son Night are true too.

The details of this story that I found most difficult to write were the parts about the narrow attitudes towards intellectually disabled people and those with mental illnesses. Today we know so much more and we do not use negative words to describe other people and we know that there is nothing to fear from those who suffer from mental illnesses or other disabilities. I also had worries using expressions like 'a touch of the tar brush' and 'savages'. But ignorant attitudes to different cultures and racist descriptions of Aboriginal people and immigrants were common in the 1950s.

In the early days of settlement in Australia there were a number of escaped convicts who were taken in and saved from starvation by Aboriginal people. I didn't make Major Manners an Aboriginal man because it is not my right to tell that story. But I do know that there are still thousands of Aboriginal bones in museums across the world. Maybe in another fifty years they will all have been returned to their rightful resting places.

Like Hedley Hopkins, I came to Australia on a boat. Today we have other people who have arrived in Australia on boats and a lot of them including children have been put straight into refugee camps. Next to their problems the ones I had seem so small.

What a story the people who are on the other side of the razor wire fence will have to tell one day.

When they have a voice.

Paul Jennings
December 2004

about the author

'Dear Paul Jennings,
How do you know what it's like to be me?'

A LONG TIME ago a young boy asked this question in a fan letter to Australia's biggest-selling writer of children's books. Since then, thousands of children have asked very similar questions of their favourite author. Somehow or other, this sensitive and funny man understands exactly what it's like to be a young person today. Perhaps in some ways he is still a child inside. Readers all over the world love him for it and he has sold over 7.5 million books worldwide.

Having been voted 'favourite author' by children in Australia more than forty times, it's no wonder he was named a KOALA* Legend in 2004. Adults too have recognised his work: *Unseen* won the Queensland Premier's Literary Award in 1997 for the best children's book; and for his services to children's literature, in 1995 he was made a Member of the Order of Australia and in 2001 he was awarded the Dromkeen Medal.

* *Kids' Own Australian Literature Awards*